TITLE: Code Red

AUTHOR: Joy McCullough

IMPRINT: Atheneum Books for Young Readers

ON-SALE DATE: 6/13/23

ISBN: 9781534496262

FORMAT: hardcover

PRICE: $17.99

AGES: 8 up

PAGES: 240

Also by Joy McCullough

Across the Pond
A Field Guide to Getting Lost
Not Starring Zadie Louise

JOY McCULLOUGH

CODE RED

Atheneum Books for Young Readers

New York   London   Toronto   Sydney   New Delhi

atheneum

ATHENEUM BOOKS FOR YOUNG READERS

An imprint of Simon & Schuster Children's Publishing Division

1230 Avenue of the Americas, New York, New York 10020

This book is a work of fiction. Any references to historical events, real people, or real places are used fictitiously. Other names, characters, places, and events are products of the author's imagination, and any resemblance to actual events or places or persons, living or dead, is entirely coincidental.

Text © 2023 by Joy McCullough

Jacket illustration © 2023 by Mary Kate McDevitt

Jacket design by Rebecca Syracuse © 2023 by Simon & Schuster, Inc.

All rights reserved, including the right of reproduction in whole or in part in any form.

ATHENEUM BOOKS FOR YOUNG READERS is a registered trademark of Simon & Schuster, Inc. Atheneum logo is a trademark of Simon & Schuster, Inc.

For information about special discounts for bulk purchases, please contact Simon & Schuster Special Sales at 1-866-506-1949 or business@simonandschuster.com.

The Simon & Schuster Speakers Bureau can bring authors to your live event. For more information or to book an event, contact the Simon & Schuster Speakers Bureau at 1-866-248-3049 or visit our website at www.simonspeakers.com.

Interior design by Rebecca Syracuse

The text for this book was set in TK.

Manufactured in the United States of America

TKTK FFG

First Edition

2 4 6 8 10 9 7 5 3 1

CIP data for this book is available from the Library of Congress.

ISBN 978-1-5344-9626-2

ISBN 978-1-5344-9628-6 (ebook)

For Jessica Lawson

Chapter One

This cannot be happening.

I must have zoned out during Mr. Trent's ramble about the Battle of Gettysburg, and I can't even blame it on an intense training session or a red-eye back from a gymnastics meet the night before. Last night all I did was stare at YouTube and try to ignore the fact that my friends were all on the way to Classics.

But when I catch up to the rest of the class, everyone is staring out the window at the school parking lot, probably alerted by Tyler, who is extremely excited about the "sweet ride" that just pulled in.

My mom's sweet ride.

Sure enough, those are my mom's red-soled high heels stepping out of the Porsche, my mom's impeccable suit, perfectly coiffed hair, pristinely made-up face.

"Isn't that your mom?" Kaia asks.

Of course it is. No one else's mom looks like that here in the Seattle suburbs, where the moms go without makeup and let their hair go gray and wear their nice yoga pants to school functions.

School functions.

Even Mr. Trent is distracted by the car, and also maybe by the appearance of my instantly recognizable mother.

"Go ahead, Eden," he says. He probably thinks someone died.

I'm starting to hope that's why she's here, even if I know it's not.

The principal cornered me on the very first day of school to ask me to invite my mom to speak at Career Day. And of course she'd ask—my mom is a high-powered executive, philanthropist, one of the most recognizable faces in Seattle.

I said she'd be out of town.

It seemed plausible. Most people assume my mom travels all the time. But flying on airplanes is the one thing she can't do. So she has people who travel for her, and she reigns supreme here in Seattle.

Kind of ironic that she married a pilot. But then maybe it makes sense why she divorced him.

Anyway, the principal didn't know that about the airplane phobia, so I figured I was in the clear. Until a minute ago.

I hurry through the hallway toward the main office, trying to convince myself someone did die. Not Dad, obviously, and not Grandma. No one in our family. Maybe, like, a distant cousin. She'd totally interrupt her workday to come pull me out of school and tell me a distant cousin had died.

That actually seems more plausible than interrupting her workday to come talk to a bunch of middle schoolers.

"Well, there she is," Principal Grady says as I burst into the front office. I can't read her face and honestly don't even care if she knows I lied to her. I have much bigger problems right now.

"Mom? What are you doing here?"

It's every bit as mortifying as I expected. It's complete justification for my lie. I knew what it would mean for my mom to speak at Career Day. If anything, I underestimated the horror.

"So remember, girls," she says, when her speech is finally over and I'm nothing but a puddle of embarrassment melding with the other mysterious stickiness on the auditorium floor, "when it's your time of the month, you'll never be caught by surprise if you keep a stash of MySecret period products in your locker!"

Over the past two years of doing online school to accommodate my training schedule, sometimes I'd think wistfully about regular-kid school things, like talent shows or field days. But clearly I left off in elementary school and couldn't conceive of the horrors middle school would bring. I couldn't conceive of my mother telling an auditorium full of my peers to fill their lockers with her company's period products.

Last I saw them, none of my friends at the gym had even gotten their period yet.

My days of online school and rigid training schedules ended for good a couple of months ago when I overshot a handstand on the bars and tore my labrum—a part of my shoulder that was already dicey from years of repetitive stress. If I'm honest, my gymnastics career had been on shaky ground for a while.

I woke up one morning around Christmas and swore I was an inch taller than I'd been the day before. Leotards and warm-up pants are stretchy, but soon my shoes were too small.

Gran took me shopping, cheering that I was finally out of kid-sized shoes. But I wasn't cheering. I knew what this meant. I just hoped no one else would notice.

They did. My coaches had to notice, because they had to teach me how to make adjustments for my growing body. When you suddenly shoot up three inches in a couple of months, it throws off your balance, your form, basically everything about your life as a gymnast.

I tried to shut out the chatter about how my growth would factor into my chances at the Hopes Classic. *Control this moment,* Coach Amy always said. Classics weren't until the spring.

I tried not to think about how I was suddenly the tallest girl on the team. Most gymnasts are small, but there've been some taller girls in the elites. Svetlana Khorkina. Nastia Liukin.

Sure, they're absolute prodigies and once-in-a-generation gymnasts, but why couldn't that be me? Kyla Ross grew almost five inches and still managed to dominate college gymnastics after the Rio Olympics.

"You'll never make it to the Olympics now," my mom said. At my birthday dinner a few weeks after the injury. "There's no point in continuing with gymnastics."

"Heather!" Gran said. "Why would you say such a thing?"

"I'm only being realistic, Mom. I'm not saying she did anything wrong, but she doesn't have the natural talent to overcome the height issue."

I blinked back tears, which Gran noticed. Mom didn't.

"Eden, honey," Gran said. "Maybe she's right. I don't know. But you don't have to be the best at something to enjoy doing it.

You could keep doing gymnastics."

"Don't be ridiculous, Mother," Mom said. Because to her, there's absolutely no point in doing something if you aren't the best there ever was. "Maybe it's not too late to pivot to ballet. Or modeling. Though you might not be tall enough for that."

I do my best to ignore the snickers on my way to lunch after the rest of the parents talk about their normal jobs. Most of the girls avoid looking at me. Some of the boys do too.

But Graham Townsend knocks my shoulder walking past, half coughing, half speaking into his hand, "Bloody Mary." His minions explode with laughter.

It doesn't make any sense, but that doesn't matter to guys like Graham. I roll my eyes and keep walking. In the cafeteria I sit at the edge of a table of girls I was kind of friends with in elementary school, even though my real friends were at the gym even then.

Two tables over, Graham shouts, "Oh, man! I got a paper cut. Hey, Eden, do you have anything to absorb the blood?"

Summer giggles, but her twin, Kaia, rolls her eyes. "Ignore him," she says. Maybe to support me, or more likely so he won't make a target of the whole table.

"I can't believe you asked your mom to come." Miranda flips her bangs out of her eyes. "Bold."

Which might be a compliment, except it isn't.

"I wouldn't let our dad come, and he's only a dentist," Summer says.

I don't say anything. Normally, I'd make small talk about their activities—Summer plays soccer, Miranda does theater, and Kaia's in student government. But I don't want anyone to ask me about gymnastics, so instead, I sit there and dream of transferring to a school where no one knows me (and more important, no one knows my mom).

Chapter Two

When the end-of-school bell finally rings, I duck into the library and hide in a back corner, pretending to be super interested in the Industrial Revolution until I'm pretty sure the hallways have cleared out.

Already today I've dealt with Graham in the hallway, Graham in the cafeteria, one of Graham's doofus friends asking Señora Waisman how to say "blood" and "month" and "stain" in Spanish, and Graham in PE telling Coach Collins he couldn't run laps because he "has cramps," and then jostling me as he and his friends lapped me on the track.

So the nearly empty hallways are a relief as I head to my locker before walking home. At least until—

"What's up, Bloody Mary?"

I'm struck with a longing to be small enough, not only for competitive gymnastics, but to climb into my locker and shut myself up tight where Graham can't reach me.

But even inside, his voice would seep through the cracks. And why should I be the one to disappear? He's the one being an immature jerk.

"Are you calling me Queen Mary Tudor, Graham? Because you should know she had, like, three hundred people executed."

He blinks, stunned for a second that I've responded, and then he's back in the game.

"Was that a threat?" he asks with a grin. "Threat of violence!" he announces to the empty hallway. "I know you've been out of school for a couple of years, but you should know that Sotomayor Middle School has a very strict zero tolerance policy for violence."

"Cool. Thanks for the info."

I slam my locker and turn to move past him, but he doesn't let me. I'm cornered.

"Graham, can you just move?"

He flails his arms up and down. "See? I'm moving! I mean, I'm not moving like an Olympian. But neither are you, I guess."

I clench my jaw. If I wait it out, he will eventually stop.

"No more special treatment for you, right?" He takes a step closer.

Gymnasts don't have very strong senses of personal space—we're super used to coaches and massage therapists and chiropractors all up in our business making adjustments, and to being packed together in locker rooms and warm-up areas with other gymnasts. But Graham is not a coach or fellow gymnast. He is not invited into my space.

"Guess you'll have to . . . what? Go into the family business?" He steps even closer. His breath is hot on my face.

"Back off," I warn him. He doesn't. "Get away from me," I say more forcefully, shoving his shoulder at the same time I hear someone else say, "Leave her alone!"

Next thing I know, Graham is howling on the ground, clutching his arm.

I look up to see a girl I don't know staring down at Graham in shock. We lock eyes.

"I barely touched him," we say at the same time.

"I pushed his shoulder—"

"I pulled his elbow—"

We come to a decision over Graham's howls. "I'll get help," I say. "You stay with him?"

I got the better end of the deal, I think, as I sprint for the main office, leaving the other girl hovering over Graham, grimacing at him with what I think is supposed to be a supportive smile as he rolls around on the floor.

I can't help but wonder if he's like those male soccer players who throw themselves to the ground the second there's a hint of a foul, only to pop back up the second the call is made. They wouldn't last a day in elite gymnastics, where we play through injuries until someone makes us stop. Graham wouldn't last a minute.

But he might actually be injured, since he keeps up the hysterics all the way through the nurse's exam, his mother's near immediate arrival, and I might even hear his wails as she straps him into the car.

Now he's off to urgent care, and I sit on the bench outside Principal Grady's office next to my accomplice, whose name is Maribel.

Principal Grady has made it clear we are not to move from this spot until our mothers arrive to speak with her. I could be sitting here for a while. My mom already took time from work to come to school once today. There's no way she's going to come back for this.

Maribel doesn't seem worried. "What was his problem?" she asks when the receptionist steps away for a break.

"Graham? He's a jerk."

"Oh, I know. He was in our fourth-grade class."

My eyebrows shoot up. Graham was in my fourth-grade class. I should probably know her.

"But he was being an extra-special jerk to you. I was . . . listening for a while. Not in like a creepy way. I just didn't want to jump in if you had it under control. But I also didn't want to leave you alone with him."

"Thanks." I sigh. "My mom spoke at Career Day—"

"Yeah, Heather Sorensen from MySecret, right?"

My heart sinks. Here this girl seemed like nongymnastics friend potential.

But her smile seems genuine. "I liked her talk."

"Really?"

"Of course. She's an amazing visionary. Total goals. And I get that Graham was being a turd about what she does, but that can't be all."

I guess if I think about it, she's right. That's not all. "I mean, it's stupid," I say. "I hadn't even thought about it until right now. But back in . . . fourth grade, I think? He had this crush on me."

"Gross."

"Yeah. That was my response. I wasn't mean, I don't think! But I shut him down."

"And he's been a turd to you ever since."

"I guess? I've honestly never noticed."

"To be fair, you don't notice much."

I turn to her in surprise. "Sorry," she laughs. "I didn't mean that how it sounded. Just, did you know we went to Salmon Springs together?"

I don't get the chance to answer because a woman who can only be Maribel's mom comes bursting through the doors. She looks like a normal Seattle mom: gray-streaked black hair in a no-fuss ponytail wearing nice yoga pants and a hoodie, with skin a couple of shades darker than Maribel's. She probably drives a hybrid minivan.

"Mija, are you all right?"

Maribel nods, standing up.

"Where's Principal Grady?"

The principal appears in the doorway, glancing at her watch. "In here. Still no word from your mom, Eden?"

I shake my head.

Principal Grady purses her lips tight, making a decision. Finally, she says, "All right, why don't the three of you come in?"

I stand up too, but before I can go into the office, Maribel's mom puts her hand on my shoulder. "Are you okay?" she asks me.

I nod, unsure how to respond.

"Okay, well, I'll have your back in there."

With that, she marches us into the office, shutting the door behind her.

Chapter Three

To my surprise, Principal Grady gives us a warm smile when we sit down. Or maybe the smile is for Maribel's mom.

"It's good to see you, Silvia," she says. "Despite the circumstances. How are Carmen and Soledad?"

"They're doing fine. But we can catch up another time. I'm more worried about what's happened to these two girls."

As she speaks, I notice she has a slight accent Maribel doesn't share. Principal Grady's face shifts into business mode. "What's happened to these two girls is that together they assaulted a boy who had to go to urgent care."

The look on Silvia's face is lethal. "Assaulted? Do not give me that, Monica. Did you even listen to their side of the story?"

"I did."

"And that boy—he was in Maribel's sixth-grade class. Made a game of snapping bra straps and pinching girls who didn't wear a bra."

"That . . . doesn't surprise me."

"He was very clearly harassing this young woman." Silvia turns to me. "He was, wasn't he?"

I think of his breath on my face, his body too close to mine. I nod.

"I was trying to get past him," I say in a rush. "I pushed at the same time Maribel pulled—"

"I was trying to get him off her—" Maribel interjects.

"—and he slipped," Silvia concludes. "Is there zero tolerance for accidents in this school?"

Principal Grady sighs and looks at a notification on her phone. "Well. That's Graham's mother at urgent care. He's fractured his wrist."

There's silence for a moment.

"That's unfortunate," Silvia finally says. "I don't wish the boy harm. But I still don't believe it's fair to punish the girls for defending themselves against his harassment."

Principal Grady squeezes the bridge of her nose. "I understand your position." She looks carefully at Maribel and me. "I truly do understand. And if Graham continues to harass you, I strongly encourage you to come tell me. However, the fact is, both girls put their hands on him, and it resulted in a significant injury. I have absolutely no choice but to insist on consequences."

Maribel's mom texts furiously as we sit on the half wall outside the school. We're suspended for the rest of the week, starting immediately, but of course my mom hasn't arrived for the meeting that's over now.

"She's not going to come," I'd told the principal. "I'll call a ride." Like I was about to before everything happened.

"Honey, kids can't take rideshares alone," Maribel's mom tells me, but Principal Grady waves her off. She knows I use RydeKids, a special rideshare service with drivers who've been authorized to escort kids around. It was a whole thing at my elementary school, so Mom's assistant made sure the middle school knew as soon as I started.

But Principal Grady still insisted my mom needed to call her before I could leave, and Maribel's mom won't leave me alone, even though I've spent every afternoon since I quit gymnastics alone—riding home, torturing myself with gymnastics videos, maybe doing homework, having dinner with Mom when she's home in time, and then it all begins again. But Silvia doesn't believe my mom won't show up, so she insists we wait together.

"Who's she texting?" I ask Maribel.

She shrugs. "Probably my dad. If you weren't here, she'd be ranting at me about injustice and misogyny and period poverty. Good to know she can keep it under wraps when she wants to."

If this is keeping it under wraps, I kinda want to see Silvia take the lid off. As it is, steam is blowing out her ears and her fingers are a blur.

Finally, her fingers slow. "Any word from your mom, Eden?"

I make a show of looking at my phone, even though I know she won't have texted. "Nope."

She purses her lips. "Can you call her?"

"She won't pick up."

The steam is starting up again. "Does she have an assistant or someone you can call?"

I pull up Akilah's phone number and Silvia holds her hand out for the phone. I happily give it to her. She walks a few paces away to tell my mom's assistant the situation. Halfway through, she holds the phone back out to me.

"Here," she says. "Tell Akilah you're alive and I'm not kidnapping you."

"I'm alive," I say into the phone. "I'm not being kidnapped."

Silvia takes the phone back and instructs Akilah to have Mom call Principal Grady ASAP, plus some more information about where Mom can pick me up after work.

"All right, then," she says, handing the phone back. "I think I've got time for a frozen yogurt stop before I need to be back at Casa Esperanza."

Casa Esperanza turns out to be the food pantry on Aurora that Maribel's mom runs.

At least, we enter through a food pantry, which is busy with both volunteers unloading donations and visitors picking them up just as quickly as they're set down. Silvia greets people in English, Spanish, and some language I don't even recognize, and leads us through swinging double doors back to a cramped maze of offices, storage, and meeting rooms.

"That's the library"—a tiny room with two ancient computers and shelves lined with books—"the copy room"—self-explanatory, but a fraction of the size of the copy room at MySecret—"the offices"—three overflowing desks, two of which are occupied—"and in there is the classroom. I think that's where I'll park you two. There's nothing scheduled in there this afternoon."

"Classroom?" I ask Maribel as Silvia bustles over to her desk.

"They have, like, ESL classes, childbirth prep, help doing taxes. Stuff like that."

Which explains why the posters on the wall include a diagram of the female reproductive system, an Immigrants' Bill of Rights, and a list explaining contractions in English.

"Wow. So it's a lot more than a food pantry."

"Yeah, it started with the one thing. But it's my mom, so of course it became a million other things, too. Basically, it's a one-stop shop for people who need free help with whatever."

"That's really cool. Why didn't she talk at Career Day?"

Maribel grins. "She had a meeting with the City Council that couldn't be changed. Fighting the NIMBYs who don't want a tent city in this neighborhood."

I blink slowly. I have no idea what that sentence even means.

She waves her hand, dismissing my confusion. "Never mind. Should we raid the stash of fruit snacks?"

My eyebrows shoot up. If those fruit snacks are meant for poor kids, I definitely don't think we should raid them.

"Oh, don't worry," she says. "They're mainly for distracting my littlest sister when she's stuck here during a late meeting."

Fruit snacks it is, then. I take the offered packet and inhale deeply at the shocking electric candy scent when I rip the package open. I'm trying to remember the last time I had a fruit snack.

"What?"

She fights a smile. "You really like fruit snacks, huh?"

I gulp down the one I had been savoring. "What, no. I was just thinking. About everything. Do you hang out here a lot?"

She shrugs and pulls some notebooks out of her backpack. "Way more than I'd like to. Even though I'm old enough to stay home alone now, there's not usually someone who can drive me there.

But I can walk here from school, so." She nods at my backpack. "Pull out some homework so it looks like we're busy, or else—"

"Girls!" Silvia calls as she strides past the classroom. "Come help unload a shipment."

". . . she'll put us to work," Maribel finishes.

Out in the food pantry, Maribel leads me over to the delivery. Three big boxes of items need organizing.

"Whoa." I peer into the closest box. Mega jars of peanut butter, cans of soup, boxes of rice and pancake mix are all jumbled together.

"Yeah, this came from a church that collected donations for a few weeks, so there's no telling what's in here. Most of it'll be good, but we need to check the expiration dates before we put things on shelves."

I pick up a jar of peanut butter and find the date, which is fine. "People really donate expired food?"

Maribel holds up a can of green beans. "September 2019. People mean well, but they remember the food drive on their way out the door and grab something from the back of their pantry."

I make a face. "Who even eats canned green beans?"

Maribel's expression is unreadable. "Why don't you check dates, and then set things in piles by category? I'll deliver them to shelves."

"Okay." I get started, trying to figure out the best way to organize things. I may not know where all the items go, but I want to be helpful. The pile of canned fruits and vegetables grows quickly. Also, dried beans and grains.

Maribel zooms around the room, delivering things to their shelves, clearly as familiar with this place as I was with Northwest Gymnastics Academy.

"How long has your mom been working here?" I ask, starting a pile of cleaning products, which I never would have thought to donate to a food bank. But obviously people need them.

"Since she opened it, when I was . . . five or so?"

"You have sisters, right? Do they help too?"

"Flor's only four, so she mostly gets in the way. You'll meet her when her preschool car pool drops her off. My older sisters used to help out more, but they're super busy now with high school stuff." She approaches the table for a new armful and squeals at some cans I've just set on the table. "Oooh, baby formula! Yes!"

"Baby formula's exciting?"

"Yeah, it's super expensive and it doesn't get donated too often." She grabs the cans and calls over her shoulder as she delivers them to her spot. "What do you do for fun?"

I fumble the can of corn I'm holding. "Um. I'm a gymnast." Was.

"I mean, yeah," she says, coming back for another armload. "That seems like it would have been so much fun. But, like . . . you're not doing that anymore, are you?"

I'm not. And even when I thought I had a shot at the Olympics, it was never fun. Not, like, the thing you do to get yourself out of a bad mood, or the thing that makes you laugh until your stomach hurts (though that could usually be accomplished with a few hundred crunches).

It's not that anyone was forcing me. I did gymnastics because I loved it, because I was good at it and I wanted to be more than good. I wanted to be the best. Every hour in the gym was one hour closer to achieving that.

But it wasn't fun.

"So what do you do now?" Maribel presses. "For fun."

"I don't know." I hold up several fashion magazines that are about a decade old.

"Recycling," Maribel confirms.

"What do you do for fun?" If I can get Maribel talking, I'm pretty sure I won't have to say anything for the rest of the afternoon.

"Me? Singing, dancing, theater. I like to cook with my dad, but not if any of my sisters are also helping. I love animals. I'd totally volunteer at a shelter or something if I could. For now, I watch a lot of cute puppy videos. Board games are fun, but they have to be the right ones. Not the super-intense strategy games. I like old-school stuff, like Pictionary and Apples to Apples and—oh! Also reading. But not sad books. If a parent is dead, I want no part of it. Wait, your dad isn't dead, is he?"

The look on my face as I try to process her words must not communicate that my dad is very much alive. A look of horror crosses hers.

"Oh my gosh, I'm so sorry. There's obviously nothing wrong with having a dead parent. I mean, there's a ton wrong with it! It's terrible and I'm so sorry, I—"

I hold up my hands to stop her. "Maribel, stop. My dad's not dead."

"He's not?"

"He's not."

"Oh, thank Frank."

"'Thank Frank'?"

"Oh, that's . . . just a thing I say."

She still looks sort of horrified, but also relieved, but now maybe embarrassed about her Frank thing, too, and I don't know what my face is doing but then a snort-giggle escapes, which makes her laugh, and then we're both laughing hysterically, the kind of laughing that's going to give me sore abs tomorrow.

"Eden?"

I whirl around at the familiar but out-of-place voice. "Coach Becca?" One of the assistant coaches from my gym is standing there, a shopping basket full of the items we've been unloading. She's not making a donation.

"Hi, um. Hey. It's good to—what are you—sorry, obviously you're—"

She puts me out of my misery. "Just picking up a few things. Hi, Maribel."

Maribel gives a little wave. Coach Becca must be a regular.

"We sure miss you around the gym," she says. "Some of the other girls are stepping up now, but they were a little lost without their leader for a while."

Their leader? I never felt like a leader. It felt like I was always fighting for my spot.

"Oh, that's . . . Yeah. I miss it too."

"Well, it's nice to see you having so much fun. I'm not sure I've ever heard you laugh like that." She pats her basket and gives a small smile. "I've got to get moving. We'd love if you dropped by the gym sometime."

"Sure, yeah. That'd be fun."

"Oh, Becca," Maribel says. "Did you see there's baby formula?"

Becca's eyes light up, and she disappears around a corner, in search of the high-demand item.

By the time my mom arrives, the doors have closed to customers. Maribel and I are slumped on the floor next to the diapers while Silvia calls in an order for Indian food that she plans to pick up on their way home.

"Do you like spicy food, Eden?" she asks me.

"Don't worry about me. I'll eat when I get home."

Silvia looks doubtful, like she's starting to believe I don't actually have a home. There's a tap at the front doors, and I hear Barbara, one of the other staff members, say, "I'm sorry, ma'am, we've just closed for the evening. You can come back at eight tomor—"

"I'm not here for the food pantry."

I leap to my feet at the sound of my mother's voice. There she is, looking impossibly out of place. The cost of her handbag could feed a family for a month. But, also, I can't blame Barbara. One afternoon of helping out around here has shown me that you can't always tell by looking what kind of person might need help from a food pantry. I never would have guessed that one of my coaches needed help.

"Eden, there you are." Mom sounds exasperated, like she's the one who's been waiting on me all afternoon.

Maribel jumps to her feet. "Ms. Sorensen, hi! I thought your talk today was great. I took notes."

Mom smiles. "Did you? Do you want to go into business?"

"Maybe. I don't know. I just want to be awesome. Like you."

Mom laughs, charmed by Maribel. "And are you the one who came to Eden's aid today at school?" She turns to me. "Are you all right?"

I nod. The display of concern is weird, but Mom does like to promote the idea that today's businesswoman can have it all—successful career and loving family.

"I'm fine."

"Good. Then we should head on home and not bother these nice people anymore."

I shoot a look at Silvia, who's eyeing my mom as she gets off the phone. "I need to at least thank Silvia."

Mom fires up her magnanimous face. She turns to Barbara. "Forgive me. Long day. Thank you so much for looking after—"

"That's not Silvia," I say. "Sorry, Barbara."

"No worries, dear. Thanks for your help today." Barbara, who had been on her way out, slips past Mom and out into the dark parking lot.

"You must be Heather." Silvia's voice is genuinely warm, unlike some people's. "I'm Maribel's mom. It's nice to meet you."

"Silvia, thank you so much for your help this afternoon." Then, to my utter horror, she pulls out a checkbook. "What do I owe you?"

"Mom!"

Silvia doesn't miss a beat. "If anything, I owe you. Eden worked very hard today." Silvia hands Mom a brochure for Casa Esperanza. "My number's on the bottom there. She's welcome here anytime."

"That's very kind of you." Mom writes a check anyway, which she leaves on the counter. "A donation for the food pantry, then. Nice to meet you all. Come on, Eden." She heads out the door.

"I have to get my stuff," I mutter to her back, then hurry to the classroom. "Thank you so much," I say to Silvia on my way back out. "For having me here this afternoon."

For supporting me at school and standing up for me to Principal Grady like my own mother wouldn't, I don't say.

Silvia smiles. "You really are welcome here anytime, Eden."

Maribel gives me a tiny wave, her face unreadable again.

Mom says nothing in the car on the way home. It isn't unusual for her not to speak to me in the car, but usually she's talking business into her Bluetooth headset. All is quiet on the menstrual products front right now, apparently.

I absentmindedly stare at my phone. There's a text from my dad.

Love you, E-girl. Taking flight.

He sends a text every time he takes off, and every time he lands. It started when I was really little, but old enough to understand what a pilot does and old enough to be freaked out that the plane was going to fall out of the sky. You'd think I'd rather not know when he was going to be flying, but I liked it better than the uncertainty of not knowing when he'd left the safety of Earth.

"Dad's taking off," I say, just to say something.

"Paris," is all she says in response.

At home, Blizz is freaking out, alerted to our arrival by the sound of the garage door. He's a blur of white, circling me as I try to get inside. I don't blame him—the dog walker comes around noon and it's almost seven.

"Come here, Blizz." He zooms ahead of me to the back door as I watch where I step. There's a solid chance he hasn't been able to hold it this long. I slip out onto the back patio and sink into one of the lounge chairs while he runs out to do his business in the grass.

Mom's silence isn't quite what I expected: a lecture on middle school being the training ground for high school, and high school determining college, and college determining life. Or a lecture about how the injured boy's parents could decide to sue us, because she's always getting sued for something or other. Or a lecture about how no daughter of hers is going to hang out in a food bank.

I don't know. Something. I didn't expect her to actually care what happened to me today. But I did expect her to care about something. Not just disappear to her room like usual.

Once Blizz has done his thing, we head back inside, where I feed him and then take my pick of the takeout in the fridge. I choose Indian. Maybe I can pretend like I'm still hanging out with Maribel's family.

The kitchen feels cold and lonely, all gleaming stainless steel and spotless countertops. Instead of sitting alone at a table for eight, I take my food to my room, resolved to bring the dirty containers downstairs before I go to sleep.

I always intend to. But if I'm honest, I'm lucky we have a housekeeper who comes a couple of times a week and clears my room of dishes.

I talked to a sports psychologist once who was weirdly happy to hear that I'm kind of a slob, in my private spaces, anyway. *You have so much control elsewhere,* she said. *It's healthy that you have some places where you let loose.*

I used to quote her to Mom when she'd get on my case about the state of my room. But it kind of feels like I can't use that excuse anymore, now that I'm not in regimented training.

When Mom sticks her head in my doorway around nine, she does survey my mess and sigh. But this time she doesn't comment on it. Blizz has finally chilled out, sprawled on top of me in my beanbag chair (on top of a pile of discarded clothes). I instinctively put my finger to my lips in a gesture of don't-wake-the-baby.

Mom scowls at the fluff ball. Honestly, a pure white designer dog seems perfectly on-brand for her. Maybe Dad actually kept her in mind when he picked Blizz out as my birthday present. Or maybe they weren't married long enough for him to realize she hates dogs.

But because she doesn't want to wake Blizz up any more than I do, she keeps her voice low. "I'll be gone by seven tomorrow," she says. "So you'll have to call a car to get to school."

Unbelievable. "Mom. I'm suspended, remember?" Did she even listen to the million messages in her voice mail?

Something flits across her face, and she pinches the bridge of her nose. "Right. Sorry. Well, I guess you'll be here, then. Olga will be here until noon, if you need anything."

"Okay."

She's about to close the door but pops her head back in at the last second. "I'm sorry I couldn't make it to school this afternoon. I was on a conference call with all the global team leaders, and I knew you could handle yourself."

I nod and sink my fingers into Blizz's fur as Mom closes the door behind her. When he's awake, the yappy little furball drives me bonkers. But there's nothing quite like his soft warmth and steady heartbeat, the way he trusts me with his silky tummy all up in the air. He's so small and vulnerable. Anything could hurt him. I won't let it.

He is my responsibility, after all.

Chapter Four

I have nowhere to be all day long, so of course I wake up at six thirty. That used to be sleeping in for me, actually, when I did two-a-day workouts with online school in the middle. I lie in bed as still as possible. The moment I move a muscle, Blizz will activate, doing back handsprings on my face, demanding breakfast. I'm staying in bed at least until Mom has left.

Eventually, I have to scratch my nose, though, and then the Blizzard is in full activation mode. He's cute, all excited like this, but I also know from previous experience that a full bladder and activation mode do not combine well.

I drag myself from bed and trip on my backpack on the way to the door. I'm hoping maybe Blizz will zip downstairs and Mom will let him out. Or our housekeeper, Olga, if she's arrived yet. But the little maniac isn't going anywhere without me. I'm the one who feeds him.

I head down the stairs on gymnast-light feet. I probably don't even need to worry about Mom hearing me—she'll be listening to some finance podcast while doing her makeup. But I feel a little thrill of triumph when Blizz and I reach the back door without encountering her.

Blizz yips at me, mad I'm asking him to go outside before I feed him. But I'm not taking any accident chances. Plus, it gives me a chance to clear the sleep cobwebs from my brain as I stand on the porch waiting for Blizz to pee.

In the kitchen I fill his dish and then pour myself a bowl of cereal, which I take back with me to my room. Curled under my covers against the persistent spring chill, my mind wanders to Maribel's family. What's her house like at seven in the morning? She's got sisters—three, I think. They're probably all busy getting ready for school, and her mom's probably reminding them about homework or lunches or after-school activities. They probably all pile into the hybrid minivan together, even Maribel, who's going with her mom to Casa Esperanza.

"Good morning, Eden."

I startle as Blizz jumps back on my bed and Olga fills my doorway.

"Are you sick today? Do you need anything?"

I set my cereal bowl on the nightstand and pull Blizz into my arms. "No, Olga, thanks. I'm not sick."

She narrows her eyes at me in a way I used to think meant she was judging me, but I have come to realize she's only trying to understand these strange people whose house she cleans. I get it. I don't understand us either.

"I do your laundry today," she says, heading for my basket.

"No, you're not supposed to."

We might have a housekeeper, but my mom's not raising a spoiled brat. I'm required to do my own laundry. Considering I'm home on a school suspension, a normal parent would probably have given Olga the day off and had me clean the whole house. My mom isn't going that far.

"But you're"—she waves her hand at my condition—"unwell."

"I'm not unwell, I promise."

She finally leaves without the laundry basket, but the next time I go downstairs, she's made me tea with honey and lemon and is picking up Blizz deposits in the backyard, which is also definitely my job.

At least Mom remembered to cancel the dog walker. After staring blankly for hours at some show I've seen a million times before, I finally rouse myself from the couch and call for Blizz, who appears instantly.

I leash him up and head outside. Our route is quieter than normal—no early morning or early evening walkers out in the middle of the day. Only the occasional dad with a jogging stroller or an older woman plodding along.

We turn down a path that looks like a private driveway but isn't. It actually leads to one of the many little hidden parks throughout Seattle neighborhoods that you don't know are there unless you know they're there.

I hadn't explored any of them before Blizz came along. Mostly I was too busy for meandering walks. And also, I didn't have a little furball of energy (and pee) who needed to get outside regularly.

Over the past few months, I've become an expert in the parks that are walkable from our house. This one has a steep, unkempt trail that zigzags down to the water, though I almost never go all the way down. The way back up is rough, especially carrying a diva dog who's decided he's done for the day.

Today, though, I have nothing but time. We can come back up as slowly as we want. So we pick our way down and make it to the rocky little beach at the bottom.

The water of Puget Sound laps quietly at the pebbled beach. Blizz runs toward the water, then startles away as it moves toward him. I let him off his leash, since the only place to go is back up the path, and I know he won't attempt that without me.

I settle on a piece of driftwood and stare out at the water. Beaches on TV are always white sand and giant waves like the ones in San Diego, where my dad's parents live, but to me they'll always be barely there waves and pebbles and driftwood and the occasional ferry moving slowly across the water.

My phone buzzes with a text: Taking flight, E-girl. Love you.

My dad landed in Paris early this morning, and now he's off again. I'm not sure how much of an adventure it feels like when flying is your job. And maybe I should be over the idea since my dad's been a pilot my entire life, but it still seems glamorous to me. Always on the move, seeing the world, more time in the air than on the ground. My dad's childhood bedroom is untouched, like a shrine, and it's filled with model airplanes and posters of fighter jets. He's doing exactly what he dreamed of from the time he was little.

It almost makes it worth it that he barely sees his kid.

Even when Olympic gold was my dream, I knew it couldn't be my life. A gymnast's career is super short. After that, maybe you're a coach. Sometimes a commentator, like Nastia Liukin. But usually you move on. Kerri Strug works for the Justice Department. Amy Chow is a pediatrician. Laurie Hernandez and Shawn Johnson became ballroom dancers!

But gymnastics was my life for as long as I can remember, and now I have no idea what my life is.

I should be more like Blizz, who doesn't think past his next meal. He's found something worth rolling around in, which means he's going to need a bath later, but in this moment it's super cute, so I snap a picture and send it to my dad for when he lands.

A minute later the rain starts, which is going to make the bath even more necessary. "Okay, Mr. Blizzard. What do you say? Should we make our way back up the path?"

I was determined to go slow and not have to carry him this time, but with the rain picking up, I just want to get home. We're both exhausted and I'm carrying a muddy dog when we reach the house. Which is locked.

No big deal. I ring the doorbell, waiting for Olga to open it. When she doesn't, I check the time with a sinking feeling. It's after noon; she's not here anymore.

Why didn't I bring keys? I walk Blizz all the time, I come home from school alone, I am not new at this. But I am new to walking Blizz in the middle of a school day. I'm off my routine, and Olga was home when I left, so I didn't think. I just acted.

Sort of like when I shoved Graham in the shoulder.

The rain is coming down hard now. I make my way around the

side of the house, carrying muddy Blizz, who is absolutely refusing to walk another step. Could Olga have left the back door open?

Of course not. Mom would freak.

This is where it would be good for us to have one of those garden-gnome key-hider things, but that would be tacky and tacky is a fate worse than death. Okay, Coach would tell me to focus on the moment. The moment includes freezing rain, a muddy dog, and an increasingly insistent bladder (mine, not his). My options are (1) staying cold and muddy for hours until my mom comes home, and peeing behind the hydrangea when nature calls, and (2) finding a way into the house.

Dad's in the air, so I text Grandma Jean.

Does Mom keep a spare key anywhere?

Her reply is, as usual, near instant. She spends almost all day in the recliner that takes up half her trailer, playing word games on her phone.

Shoot if I know. You locked out, punkin?

Grandma doesn't drive or live close enough to walk, so there's nothing she can really do to help me.

I'll figure it out. Thanks.

I circle the house, looking for open windows. For once Blizz doesn't follow me. Instead, he sits shivering at the door, looking at me like I've betrayed him somehow.

Of course no windows are open. It's April in Seattle. Everything's blooming and trying to convince you it's spring, but the air still holds on to the chill of winter, most days. Olga's always turning up the heat and telling me to put on a sweater. She's not going to leave a window open.

Except in my mom's room, because she's not allowed in there. And my mom likes to sleep cold.

I make my way to the back of the house and look up to the second-story window of my mom's room. Sure enough, it's open. There's a screen, but if it's like the one in my room, it pops out pretty easily. Still, it's on the second story, and there's the little problem of how to even reach the window.

Blizz lets out an indignant yelp. He cannot for the life of him understand why I haven't opened the door yet.

I drag the patio table underneath the window and climb on top. I've had a growth spurt, but not enough to make this home invasion easy. I consider my other options in the yard. The spinning chairs that go with the table are super unstable. But the lounge chair on the other side of the yard has a wooden-slat base. Almost . . . like a ladder.

This is so reckless. If I were in training, I would never in a million years risk the injury. But I've already torn my labrum; I'm never doing gymnastics again. Honestly, what would it even matter if I broke an arm right about now?

What do you do for fun? Maribel's question rings in my mind. Probably no one answers that question with, "Breaking and entering!" But now that the challenge has presented itself, I'm not backing down. It's a double Arabian my coach tries to cut from my floor routine because she doesn't think I can land it, but I throw it mid-routine just to show her, and even more, myself. (And maybe the tiniest bit, my mom.)

I drag the lounge chair over to the table. Thankfully, the rain has let up, but all the surfaces are slick. I've come this far, though.

I manage to get the lounge chair up onto the table and climb up after it.

Blizz has left his station at the door and barks at me from the ground.

"I know, Blizz," I say. "But my suspension was totally unjust. I might as well do something to deserve it."

With the lounge chair braced in its flattest position, I prop it against the house, and sure enough it reaches up to the window easily.

It's not a ladder, though. The wood slats are too close together to step on. I take off my sneakers and toss them to the ground. Barefoot, I can wedge my toes between the slats, gripping the outer edges of the chair with my hands. I move a few slats up and give a tiny wiggle. I don't go sprawling down to the table, so that seems like a good sign.

It's no different than standing on a beam, really. If the beam were wobbly. And rough. But if I could do a backflip while balancing on a four-inch-wide beam, four feet in the air, I can do this. Probably.

"Here goes nothing, Blizz."

He yelps with what I decide is encouragement, and I climb the rest of the way, powering through the pain in my shoulder, until I'm level with my mom's open window. I push on the screen, which gives a little, but not all the way. It's going to need more force. I let go of my ladder/lounge chair so I can push with both hands, effectively popping the screen in, but also causing my ladder to slip out from under me.

That's where my upper body strength comes in handy. I'm not

as strong as I used to be, but I'm still strong, even if my shoulder is complaining by the time I wrench myself up and over the windowsill, tumbling into my mom's room.

I land on her nightstand, knocking a lamp to the ground, which shatters as I fall off the nightstand into the broken pieces.

"Well, tomorrow will not be a repeat of today," Mom says, mercilessly yanking off my bandages because she doesn't believe I cleaned the wounds properly first.

"I know. I won't leave the house at all. I won't even leave my bedroom."

"You are not staying home alone again." She presses an antiseptic-soaked cloth to my forearm, which got the worst gash from the shards of Tiffany lamp. The Tiffany lamp that she bought with her first big paycheck from her first big job.

I gasp at the pain. "I've been home alone constantly since my injury!"

"And clearly that has had a detrimental effect on your judgment. Without gymnastics to focus you, it's like I don't even know who you are anymore!"

She's never known who I am. She just thought she did when I was following the life plan she'd set out for me.

"This was just a freak accident—"

"Freak accidents are starting to become a pattern with you, and it is my job as your mother to make sure you're safe." She spreads a clean bandage over the wound, and then pushes back from the table, striding into the hall to make a phone call.

Did she seriously just compare this accident to what happened when I defended myself against Graham? Today I maybe made some dumb choices, but what happened with Graham was not my fault.

"Look, Mom," I say, when she comes back in, but she cuts me off with a flick of her wrist.

"Eden. We're both figuring out how to adjust to this new reality where you're . . . not filling your time with gymnastics. I thought you could be trusted at home alone, but today has shown me otherwise. Be ready at eight. That woman said you were welcome anytime and I've just confirmed with her. I'll be dropping you at Casa Esperanza for the day."

The next morning I'm awake even earlier than the day before. What are you supposed to wear to work at a food bank? I don't want to look too fancy, but I also don't want to look disrespectfully schlubby. I have to dig to the bottom of the pile on my chair to find my favorite jeans, which I pair with a nice hoodie.

I take Blizz for a long walk, since I've got time and I'm hoping I'll tire him out so he'll sleep until the dog walker arrives. As much as he sometimes annoys me, it annoys me even more when Mom gets mad at him. It's not Blizz's fault my dad decided this poor dog should fill all the holes in my heart.

Mom adds money to my card for lunch and gives me a lecture about being on my best behavior, and then pulls out of the parking lot the moment Maribel opens the doors to Casa Esperanza. I hadn't been sure she'd be there, and I'm thrilled to see her.

"Hi!" she exclaims. "Thank Frank you're here! Yesterday was so boring." She links her arm through mine and pulls me through the dark food bank to the offices, which are lit up and bustling. Barbara waves to me from her desk. Another volunteer is busy in the copy room, and Silvia fidgets with an ancient coffee maker.

"Eden! Hello, dear. Any chance you're great with machines?"

I shake my head. "Oh! But I could go across the street for coffee."

She smiles. "Not in the budget. Thanks, though."

"No, I . . . my mom gave me money."

She hesitates for a moment and then shrugs. "Okay, why not? It'll be a bleak day for everyone if I don't get some caffeine in me soon."

Maribel and I take orders and then go outside. I head for the crosswalk to go across busy Aurora Avenue to the nearest Starbucks, but Maribel grabs my arm and tugs me the other way. I'm starting to see why Graham fell when she pulled his arm—girl has a grip!

"Just a block up this way, there's a better spot," she says.

She leads me to a coffee shop called Black Coffee, which is lined with warm wood paneling, the walls covered with vibrant art. It has way more personality than a Starbucks.

"This is nice."

"It's the only Black-owned coffee shop in Shoreline," she says. "And they have the best doughnuts."

Being a block away from Starbucks doesn't seem to be hurting business. The line is full of people heading in to work, and the tables are populated with people on laptops.

"What do you think they're doing?" Maribel asks as we wait.

I shrug. "I mean . . . working?"

"No, but . . . her, for example." She chin-points to a woman in her late twenties with red, curly hair and magenta lipstick, a tea-cup dog in a bag on the seat next to her. She's typing furiously into a rose-gold laptop. "What's she working on?"

I shrug again, pretty sure this is a game I don't know how to play.

"I think she's writing a romance novel," Maribel says. "One of the ones where the two main characters super hate each other in the beginning and then by the end they're head over heels in love."

I'm catching on. "How about him?" I nod toward an elderly man writing methodically in a leather-bound journal. "Love poetry," I offer. "About his late wife."

"Ooh, yes," Maribel says. "It's the only way he feels close to her."

"And he always comes here to write because this is where they met."

Maribel giggles. "I think this coffee shop has only been here, like, a few years."

Even though it's not a competition, I won't be defeated. "So? Maybe they met at the grand opening, after their tai chi for seniors class at the community center."

Maribel grins.

"Can I help you?"

We turn to the barista and Maribel reads off the list of orders.

"I'd like a chai latte," I add. "With whipped cream." I turn to Maribel. "What do you want?"

She shrugs me off. "I'm good. I have water."

I poke her with my debit card. "Seriously. It's on my mom."

She relents and orders a hot chocolate. I add a request for two doughnuts, and we move off to the side to wait for our drinks.

After we've identified someone writing a memoir about his

life as a ventriloquist, a college professor planning a lecture about Shakespeare, and someone writing a crime thriller, our drinks are ready.

By the time we bring them back to Casa Esperanza, half a dozen people are waiting outside for the doors to open.

"We'll be open in a couple of minutes," Maribel assures them as we slip inside and deliver the drinks.

"Please thank your mother," Silvia says after she inhales half her black coffee. "I promise I'm not going to make you two work all day, but are you up for a morning shift?"

Anything is better than sitting around alone in my house, and we won't have our homework assignments from our teachers until at least three.

"What can we do?"

Maribel is sent to copy some flyers about Casa Esperanza's upcoming classes. Silvia leads me out into the food pantry.

"We're about to open up," she tells me. "There'll be a lot more people than that first afternoon you were here—people trying to get their groceries before they have to be at work or drop their kids at school. Everything's free, but there are limits on how many they can take of certain items. They're posted on the shelves. If you notice someone taking more than their share, just let Barbara know.

"When Maribel gets out here, she may ask your help unloading inventory during lulls, but mostly you can be here, where people will bring their baskets, and you can help them bag their groceries. Mostly you're here to be a friendly face, and to answer their questions."

I blink at her, my heart speeding up. "But I won't know the answers."

She smiles, unbothered by the completely unqualified volunteer she's letting loose in her food bank. "'I don't know, but I'll find out' is a perfectly acceptable answer, Eden."

She situates me at a folding table just as the doors open and a dozen people pile inside, beelining for specific items. One young woman stands with a baby on her hip, hanging back, clearly as new as I am.

Silvia spots her immediately and swoops in to show her the ropes. When they reach the diapers, the young woman bursts into tears of gratitude.

Silvia brings her basket over to me. "Would you bag these, Eden, and then keep them behind the counter? I'm going to take Vanessa here back for a tour."

Right as I'm finishing bagging Vanessa's groceries, Maribel appears with a multicolored stack of flyers. She lays them out on my table grouped by color, and I see that they're all the same flyer, but each in a different language.

"When people come to bag their stuff, point out the flyers about our current free classes. Don't forget to say 'free.'"

The next woman to approach the table shakes her head when I tell her about the free classes. "No English," she says.

"Okay, but . . ." I grab a few different flyers and point out the titles in different languages. None of them is her language, but she understands and finds the one she needs. Her eyes light up and she tucks the flyer into her bag.

When there's finally a lull, I tell Barbara I'm going to the bathroom and slip into the back. The young woman and her baby are still there, sitting in the library with Silvia, who plays with the baby while the young woman does something on one of the computers.

"You okay, Eden?" Silvia calls.

I nod and mouth, *Bathroom.*

It's a bathroom slash storage room, filled with boxes, and has barely enough room to maneuver. But I make it to the toilet, sit down, and see a bright red splotch on my underwear.

Okay then.

I know what periods are. I'm thirteen and my mom is head of one of the biggest menstrual product companies in the world. So I'm unprepared to feel kind of . . . shocked. Like I somehow knew it was coming and yet never expected it to happen to me?

Gymnasts get their periods later, mostly. Strenuous training regimens and low body-fat percentages mean your body knows it's not a hospitable place to host a baby, so it holds off on releasing eggs. Not that my body is going to host a baby anytime in the next decade, but I watched the uncomfortable videos about puberty in my homeschool curriculum. That's what periods are—your body deciding it's developed enough for that stage of life.

But I'm not training anymore, so I'm losing muscle. Which means my body has apparently decided it's time to shed some uterine lining.

It's kind of no big deal and also a huge deal. The ads for my mom's company make it seem like it's such a hassle, like it interrupts your life so much (unless you use MySecret!), like it's this huge, painful burden. A burden I'll have to deal with once a month for decades.

But the main thing right now is the fact that there's a splotch of blood in my underwear, and even though sometimes my life feels like one never-ending commercial for MySecret pads and tampons, I don't have one on me now.

I wad up a bunch of toilet paper and stick it in there to collect whatever else is coming. It's bulky and awkward when I stand up. But thankfully the splotch didn't stain my jeans. Hopefully, I'll be okay until I get home and break into my first pink, sparkly box of MySecret products.

I consider asking Silvia if she has anything better, but she's still helping Vanessa and her baby in the library.

Back in the food bank, Marisol has taken over my spot at the flyer table. I've just joined her when a tall girl with streaks of hot pink through her curly black hair comes in with her arms full of takeout bags.

"Finally!" Maribel exclaims. "I'm starving!"

This strikes me as a pretty rude way to treat a delivery person, but then Maribel runs up to her, takes the bags, and says, "You left eye shadow all over the sink again."

Maribel disappears into the back with the bags and the older girl turns to me. "Hi. Are you a new volunteer? I'm Soledad."

"Maribel's sister?" I guess. "I'm Eden."

"Oh!" Her eyes light up, and honestly, however much eye shadow she left on the sink was worth it because her makeup is a work of art. "Her suspension buddy! Way to stand up for yourself with that jerk boy."

"Oh. We didn't mean to—"

"Eden!" Maribel sticks her head back out front. "Come back for lunch. Sol, mind the front."

I shoot an apologetic look toward Soledad, but she doesn't even notice. She's already straightening the flyers.

She's brought a hodgepodge of Korean food, which Silvia and Barbara are unloading on the table in the classroom. "Help yourself, Eden," Silvia says. "You've been working hard."

"Oh, thank you. How much do I owe you?"

She waves me away. "It's a donation. Mr. Gyeong relied on the food bank when it was first opened, and now that he's got a successful restaurant, he sends over lunch once a week."

"Oh. Cool. Thanks." I take a seat and help myself to a scallion pancake. But I've only had a few bites before I feel a weird sensation, sort of like I'm peeing, but not, and I have no control over it. I shift, super aware that the folded-up toilet paper I stuck in my underwear is not enough.

"Um. Excuse me."

I back out of the room like I'm the subject of a queen I can't turn my back on and then zip into the bathroom. It's way worse than before—the blood has soaked through my jeans. What am I supposed to do? I've got all afternoon left here. I can't walk around with a giant bloodstain on the back of my pants, and obviously, wadded-up toilet paper is not going to do it.

I'm frozen, unsure what to do. I sit there for the longest time, until finally I hear a knock on the door.

"Eden? Are you okay?"

I mean, yes? No? I don't know. This is a weird situation. But Maribel is the one kid who didn't make fun of me for having a mom who runs a menstrual products company. She even said she was "total goals" and kissed up to her when she picked me up the first day.

or one.

"If I wanted to put myself out there," Mom says, stabbing a
t aby potato with her fork, "it would not be with Scooter Jenkins!"

Gran sighs and turns to me. "How about you, Eden? Did you
nd that spare key you were looking for?"

That sets Mom off again, telling Gran all about my break-in,
r d my "community service"—her words—at Casa Esperanza,
ch leads to explaining my suspension.

"Suspended? My Eden? Why on Earth was she suspended?"

'She pushed a boy to the ground. Fractured his wrist."

ran's hand flies to her heart. "Whatever for?"

an freeze. What am I supposed to say? I was getting bullied
se Mom came to school and the life's work that pulled her out
or to poverty Gran still chooses to live in is deeply humiliating to

with m recovers faster than I do. "She was standing up for her-
me. had every right to. Honestly, I'm proud of her. Even if deal-

"V her suspension is a scheduling nightmare."

you tr shocked, I barely feel it as Gran takes my hand. "Do you

"Tl t your mother once turned around during a church choir
her bag ce and punched the boy who stood behind her?"

rinse the okes on a bite of potato. "He was pulling my hair!"

"Um off the riser," Gran tells me with a conspiratorial smile.

She b er, what if I told you that *Scott* owns his very own auto

A cup.

The ne

get Barbar

now. This m

speech.

Chapter Six

Mom drops me at Casa Esperanza early the next morning. So early that the windows are dark and the doors are locked. I knock on the door.

"What do you think?" Mom calls from the car, clearly itching to get moving.

"I'm sure they'll get here soon," I say. "You can go."

Mom hesitates. It's not the poshest part of town.

"I could go wait in the coffee shop," I suggest.

Mom nods with relief. "That sounds good. I'll see you later."

But as soon as her car pulls away from the curb, a battered old van pulls into the spot she left. I might be nervous I'm about to be abducted, except that the van is covered in kitschy-cute stickers—rainbows and unicorns and glittery stars. Of course, come to think of it, that might be the perfect van to entice small children. . . .

"Eden, hey!"

It's not a kidnapper who opens the passenger side door but

Will, Maribel's friend from yesterday. Raven hops out of the driver's side and comes around to slide open the van door.

"Hi, Eden," she says. "Want to help unload?"

I take the plastic bin she offers. "They're not here yet," I say over my shoulder as I haul it toward the door.

"We've got a key." Will tosses a set of keys into the air and then misses them on their way back down. He grins sheepishly as he recovers them and unlocks the door.

Raven joins us, juggling multiple cloth totes and a sewing machine. Inside, she heads back to the classroom and we follow with the bins.

"They told me you make pads," I say as Raven sets up her sewing machine on the main table. "But I didn't know you did it here."

"I don't, normally. But there's construction by our building and the power is out today. I've got a big order to finish, so Silvia said I could set up here."

Will's opened one of the plastic bins and is setting out already-cut pieces of fabric in an assembly line next to his mom.

The front door chimes.

"There's our fearless leader," Raven says with a grin.

"Hello?" Silvia calls from the front.

I step into the hall, but before I can take another step, I collide with a whirlwind of glitter and tulle. The small, sparkly person bounces off me and spins into the classroom, where she flings herself into Will's arms.

"Will! Will! Will!" she shrieks. "Why did you leave? Never go away again!"

Will and Raven both laugh. "Hey, Flor," Will says.

She jumps out of his arms, indignant, arms crossed over a pile of costume jewelry weighing down her tiny frame. "My name is not Flor!"

"Since when?"

"Since I changed it from boring Flor to . . . Chrysanthemum!"

Before anyone can question this, she whirls around and turns on me. "Who are you?"

"Rude, Flor," comes Maribel's voice from the doorway. "This is my friend Eden. I told you about her."

"I believe she goes by Chrysanthemum now," Will says, earning himself a flurry of hugs and kisses from Maribel's youngest sister.

"Okay, fine," Maribel says. "But last week it was Delphinium, so it's a little hard to keep up." Maribel rolls her eyes at her sister's huff of indignation. "Eden, come up front."

I follow Maribel out to the food bank room, and Will and Flor/Chrysanthemum trail behind us. Silvia greets me warmly and then leaves us to unload some newly delivered supplies.

"Did you hear about Graham?" Maribel says while her sister talks Will's ear off.

"What? No." I have no way of hearing anything about school, since I'm not really texting friends with anyone there.

"Oh my gosh, apparently he's been playing volleyball in PE with his 'fractured' wrist."

"What?"

"Don't tell my mom, though. She'll march in there and demand we be unsuspended." She pauses, and suddenly looks a little nervous. "I mean, this is way more fun than school, don't you think?"

"Absolutely."

When I go back for a bathroom break, I grab a pad from my back-pack in the classroom. Raven's got a small stack of completed pads at her side, and her sewing machine hums along happily.

When I'm done in the bathroom, I pause in the doorway, watching Raven sew. The sound of the machine brings me back so vividly to a time before MySecret, or at least to its earliest stages. Mom had already started the company when she got pregnant with me, but she wasn't going to let a little thing like motherhood stop her.

Still, it stayed small for a few years, which meant she had time for me and for hobbies. Which included sewing. She used to make me clothes—copies of the expensive stuff she couldn't dream of affording. I think she made clothes for herself, too. But I haven't seen her sewing machine in years.

"Do you sew?" Raven asks, pausing to adjust something on her machine.

"No. My mom used to."

"Well, we can always use more volunteers," Raven says. She reaches into one of her bins of supplies and pulls out a business card. "Tell her to check out the website!"

I look at the card. PERIODS WITH DIGNITY, it says in bold letters. And then, in smaller letters: PROVIDING REUSABLE SUP-PLIES AND TRAINING TO MENSTRUATORS AROUND THE GLOBE. There's a phone number, an email address, and a website my mom will definitely never check out.

"Cool, thanks."

"Anytime," she says, turning back to her work.

"And thanks again. For yesterday."

She blinks, confused. Then she remembers. She's probably given so many pads to so many people in need that yesterday was nothing to her.

"Of course, Eden. Anytime."

"Do you still have your sewing machine?" I ask my mom as we clean up after dinner.

"My sewing machine?"

"Didn't you used to sew? When I was little?"

Now that I say it out loud, it sounds ridiculous. My mother, sewing? Maybe I had one of those dreams that are so vivid, they feel real. Maybe I made it up entirely.

But a smile melts across Mom's face. "I did," she says. "And I do still have it. Why?"

I explain about Raven sewing at Casa Esperanza today, though for some reason I leave out the part about her reusable menstrual pads. I shrug, like I don't really care one way or another.

"It seemed kind of fun," I say.

Mom leads me down to the basement, kicking off her heels before she climbs the steep stairs. I follow her down into the dark, dusty space lit only by the light streaming in the small windows at either end. She starts pulling storage containers aside until she's got three bins in the center of the room.

"Help me get these upstairs," she says.

We haul them into the guest bedroom. The first bin contains the sewing machine, along with some boxes filled with scissors and thread and zippers, and other random things I can't identify. The second bin is filled with fabric of all sorts of colors and prints. And from the third bin she pulls a mannequin torso.

A dress form, she calls it as she shows me how I can spin little dials to adjust the size of the waist, the bust, the hips to make the dress form match the size of the person I'm sewing for.

I don't think size matters when sewing menstrual pads, but she's so excited that I don't mention that.

"Do you want me to show you the basics?" she asks, plugging in the machine.

"Sure."

She pulls a scrap of fabric from the bin and settles at the desk, while I sit on the edge of the bed watching over her shoulder. She shows me how to put a spool of thread on its perch at the top of the machine, and another mini-spool of thread (which she calls a bobbin) in a little compartment down below. Then she sandwiches the piece of fabric between a metal plate and this thing that comes down snug on top of it, and makes the needle jump up and down by pressing a pedal with her foot.

"See," she says. "You can adjust the stitch length here. It's a pretty simple machine, but the newer ones are all computerized and can do a ton of different stitches. If you're interested in sewing, we could get you—"

"This one looks great," I tell her. "Can I try?"

We switch places, and I give the pedal an experimental press. It zooms along so quickly, I veer off the fabric. This was stupid. I should have known it wouldn't be as easy as it looked.

But for once, Mom isn't critical. She just says, "You don't have to press so hard," and helps me readjust the fabric and try again.

By the time she's ready to turn in for an early morning, I'm still trying to master straight lines. Coach would tell me to give this skill a chance to settle in, drilling it over and over before I increase the difficulty. But I'm like a gymnast who does her first standing back tuck and wants to immediately try it on the beam.

And once I've mastered sewing two straight lines together, I'm not stopping there. I can see the possibility. I'm making something out of nothing. Except I'm not really making something. Two scraps of fabric sewn together aren't of any use to anyone.

But the pads Raven makes and distributes to people who need them—like she did for me!—those are useful! I could make something that could rescue someone from embarrassment in school or a locker room or wherever!

I dig out the card Raven gave me for Periods with Dignity and go to the website. It's bright and welcoming, with background on how Raven started the organization, photos of Raven (and sometimes Will) in faraway places, teaching locals how to make the pads. I spot Silvia in one photo of a group of women in beautifully woven tops and skirts. "Chichicastenango, Guatemala," the caption says.

I follow the link to instructions, where it invites anyone who sews to make pads from the pattern and either send them in to Periods for Dignity, or distribute them themselves in their own communities.

The pattern prints out onto a single piece of paper, so before I know it, I have a kind of garish floral fabric—better not to use the nicest supplies on my first attempt—spread out on the floor of the guest bedroom with the pattern piece on top of it.

Cutting the fabric is a lot harder than it looks on TV fashion competitions. As soon as I try to cut the fabric, the pattern piece moves. But if I try to hold the pattern piece down, I can't position the scissors correctly.

I'm about to throw the scissors down in frustration when I hear Coach's voice in my head: *Step back. What are your options?*

That's when I remember the absolute most indispensable resource for anyone anywhere trying to learn something: YouTube. Honestly, I don't know how anyone learned to do anything before YouTube.

Sure enough, there are videos on how to cut out pattern pieces, and then videos on how to sew on a curve, and then videos on how to turn the thing I've sewn inside out and press it with the iron, so it goes from being a hideous, misshapen blob to actually being recognizable as a pad. Sure, it's a little wonky, and it took me until two in the morning, but I go to bed feeling like I've finally accomplished something.

Chapter Seven

Raven's not at Casa Esperanza the next morning.

"Her electricity must be back on," Maribel says with a shrug. "Did you get my email last night?"

"Oh, sorry. I don't check it that often. Do you want my number, so you can text next time?"

Maribel throws her head down and (lightly) bashes it against the table we're sitting at. "I. Have. No. Phone."

"Oh. Sorry. I'll try to check my email more. What were you texting about?"

"I wondered if you want to spend the night tonight. My mom already checked with yours and she said it's fine. I figured you could bring your stuff with you today, but . . ."

"Oh, shoot." I'm not sure what to think. I can't remember the last time I had a sleepover with a friend, though I did share hotel rooms with teammates at out-of-town meets. Those weren't exactly sleepovers, though. Even when something sleepover adjacent would happen, like my teammates finding karaoke on the hotel

TVs, I was the one who made them turn it off and go to bed. We had to stay healthy and get enough sleep. If I was going to get anything less than gold, it wasn't going to be because of Russell's off-key rendition of "Shake It Off."

"But we could swing you by your house to get your stuff on the way home," she says hopefully.

I have no idea what my hesitation is about. Maribel is so nice, she weirdly seems to like my mom, and every member of her family whom I've met so far is just as nice as she is. Maybe I don't want her to see my house? But it's no secret that we're rich, I guess.

"Okay," I say, and then she's squealing and throwing her arms around me like we're best friends.

Maybe we are?

Maribel's helping me with my math in the classroom when Raven arrives, later that afternoon.

"Hey, girls," she says, peeking her head in.

"Do you need us to move?" I ask.

"No, I'm good. I'm not sewing today. Just came by to discuss some travel details with Silvia."

"Travel?" I instantly picture Raven and Will and Maribel's family in an RV, going to the Grand Canyon or somewhere happy families go all together. For someone with a pilot father, I have been on surprisingly few family vacations.

"They're going to Guatemala," Maribel says.

"You're still invited, M," Raven says. "Let me know if you change your mind!"

"Guatemala? Why? Is Will going?" That's way more than an RV trip.

"It's for Periods with Dignity," Raven explains. "And, yes, Will's going. Silvia usually helps with the travel details when I'm going somewhere in Latin America, since she speaks the language better than I do. And with Guatemala she's especially helpful, since she's got family there."

I turn to Maribel. "You've got family there and you don't want to go?"

She shrugs. "I've been."

"Good to see you girls," Raven says, and ducks out of the doorway before I've gotten up the courage to show her the wonky pad I made last night.

"Why wouldn't you want to go? That sounds so cool!"

"I mean, some of it is," Maribel says. "But I hate airplanes. And I don't really speak Spanish, so I sit there not understanding while everyone chatters around me. It's lonely."

"But if Will is there . . ."

"I just don't want to go, okay?"

When we emerge from the classroom having finally vanquished graphing inequalities, Raven is still there, discussing travel details with Silvia.

Raven's so unlike any of the adults I've ever known—definitely nothing like my mom, but also nothing like any of my coaches or PTs or anyone around the gymnastics world. Her laugh is so loud, they must hear it out on the street, even with all the traffic rushing by on Aurora.

By the light of day, the pad I felt so victorious about the night before is a lumpy, misshapen blob. But even if my first attempt is completely atrocious, I have the feeling she's not going to judge me for it.

I dig the pad out of my backpack and approach. Silvia and Raven pause in their discussion and look at me.

"Sorry, I—" This was a dumb idea. I start to crumple it into my hand and back away, but Raven reaches out, a brilliantly colored peacock tattoo revealed on her inner forearm.

"What's that?"

I uncrumple the pad and Raven takes it, smoothing it out as a broad smile crosses her face. "Did you make this?"

"I know it's totally wonky. It was my first time sewing. Anything."

"Anything?" Silvia takes the pad and turns it over. "Amazing. I still can't sew a straight line."

"But you help in lots of other ways," Raven says. Then says to me in a mock whisper, "But she's right. Will's bearded dragon could sew a better seam than Silvia."

"I know it's not perfect," I say in a rush. I hate the feeling that they're humoring me, like I used to with little kids who'd show me their wobbly handstands and wait for me to tell them they were going to beat me to the Olympics. "And I didn't know how to finish it, because I didn't have whatever you need for snaps?"

"Eden, I can honestly say, this is the best first attempt I have ever seen. And if you want to make more, you can bring them to me and I'll put the snaps on later."

My cheeks flush at the praise. It's a sort of dumb thing to feel proud of, I guess, but I haven't felt like this in a while. "Okay."

"Come on," Maribel tugs on my arm. "Weren't we going to Black Coffee?"

"Yeah, sorry."

"You know," Raven says, before Maribel manages to pull me out the door. "I'm having a sew-along at my house this weekend. All day Saturday, I'll be there with friends, teaching newcomers how to make the pads. You could get some pointers and use the snap press!"

That sounds way more interesting than my existing plans for Saturday: lying on my bed watching videos in between walking Blizz. I turn to Maribel.

"Are you going?"

Maribel wrinkles her nose and Raven laughs. "I have tried and failed many times to recruit Maribel," she says. "But Will's going to be there!"

Something shifts on Maribel's face. "Maybe I could try again," she says. "It might be more fun with Eden."

"We can't," Silvia says. "Carmen has her Model UN thing in Bellingham."

Maribel rolls her eyes but smoothes her face back into neutral at a sharp glance from Silvia.

"Maybe next time," Raven says. "You know we'd love to have you, M. But, Eden, you've got my phone number on my card. Text me if you want the address. We'll start at ten and go all day!"

All afternoon, Maribel talks about how she's always being dragged to Soledad's plays and dance performances, Carmen's Model UN and debate competitions, and even little Flor's tumbling presentations.

"Don't you mean Chrysanthemum?" I say as we climb into Silvia's car.

Maribel sighs. "Fine, although I think she's going to regret that particular choice when she has to start writing it. And whatever you do, do not tell her you're like a gymnastics prodigy. You'll never shake her then."

"Where to, hon?" Silvia asks from the driver's seat.

Oh yeah. We're swinging by my house to pick up my things for overnight.

"We don't have to go all the way to my house," I say. "I'm sure I could wear something of Maribel's to sleep."

"Don't be silly," Silvia said. "You live in Richmond Highlands, right?" She turned out of the lot in the direction of my house. As we leave Aurora and head west, the houses get bigger the closer they are to the view of Puget Sound. And I get more uncomfortable.

"So Flor's into gymnastics, huh?" I say, trying to distract Maribel, like she won't notice these houses are way too big for any single family.

"I mean, she's four," Maribel says. "They're extremely advanced if they can do a cartwheel."

"Everyone starts somewhere," I say.

"Like you and that pad you sewed," Silvia says from the front. "I'm seriously so impressed. When I first met Raven, she tried to recruit me and I was a total disaster."

"My mom used to sew," I say. "So she showed me some things. Oh, turn left here."

We're closer now. There's no avoiding it. They've met my mom and seen how she waves around her checkbook, so the house isn't going to be some big shock. I only need to get in and out with my overnight things and a pit stop for Blizz, and then we'll be out of here before I can scare Maribel off.

"It's, um, just up here on the right. The drive with the red mailbox."

Silvia turns in. You can't see the house from here, since the driveway winds along a ways to where the house is perched on the overlook to the Sound.

"Whoa," Maribel says as her mom pulls up in front.

"Okay, I'll be right back." My heart sinks as Maribel follows me out of the car.

At the sound of our voices, Blizz starts to freak out inside.

"Oh my gosh, you didn't say you have a dog," Maribel squeals. "Now I have to come in! I love dogs so much, but stupid Soledad is allergic. What's its name?"

At least Blizz will distract her. I unlock the door and Blizz is unleashed, an entire weather event around our feet.

"This is Blizz. Here, let's take him through to the backyard or he'll pee all over you." I rush them through the house and deposit Maribel and Blizz in the backyard. "This is perfect. If you could keep him out here and make sure he pees, I'll get my things together and we can go."

I race up to my room and unearth a duffel bag from underneath my bed. I throw the first clothes I find into the bag, and stop by the bathroom for toiletries. When I get back downstairs, Maribel and Blizz are coming back inside.

"Your yard is amazing," Maribel says. "This house is amazing. Can I see your room?"

"I mean . . . your mom is waiting in the car?"

"And we're going to leave this precious pumpkin here all alone?" She gathers Blizz up in her arms and buries her face in the fluffy fur.

"I know. My mom will be home pretty soon." I hope. Not that she'll pay any attention to Blizz, but I don't tell Maribel that.

"I wish we could bring him to sleep over too."

Blizz would be in heaven at Maribel's house, with so many people, especially Maribel, who clearly loves him more in five minutes than I ever have.

"Yeah." I get close and pet Blizz. Every time I do, I enjoy it. He's adorable and sweet and loves me. But when I'm not with him, I don't even think about him.

Am I terrible person?

"I love you, smooshy floofball Blizzie Wizzie," Maribel says as we shut the door.

Maribel's house is closer to Casa Esperanza, in a neighborhood where most of the houses are from the 1950s or 60s, with the occasional newly constructed house plopped down in the middle of them like a football player sitting with a group of gymnasts.

The driveway Silvia pulls into is lined with overgrown lavender and rosemary bushes, and dandelions surround Flor's toys on the lawn.

Silvia sighs. "Would you move the tricycle, hon?"

Maribel pops out of the car to drag a glittery blue trike onto the grass.

"Sorry about the mess," Silvia warns me as I climb out. "It's even worse inside."

It doesn't look messy to me, though. I mean, it's nothing compared to my bedroom. Mostly, it looks warm and inviting, like a family lives here.

"Mari! Mari! Mari!" Flor squeals from the porch, where she hops barefoot from one foot to another, alternately holding each foot out. "Daddy and I painted our toenails! We're making individual pizzas for dinner! Because Eden is here!"

Maribel rolls her eyes, and tousles Flor's hair as she walks past. "I know, Flor. She's right here."

Flor's face immediately scrunches up in displeasure, but before she can complain, I say, "I like your toenails, Chrysanthemum."

She beams and takes my hand, dragging me inside. "You'll sleep in my room."

"We're actually going to sleep in the basement, monkey," Maribel says, then quickly adds, "but how about you show Eden our room now?"

I follow Flor through the living room and down a hall. "That's Sol and Carmen's room," she says, pointing at a closed door with a whiteboard covered in messages on it. "And that's Mami and Dad's room." She points to an open door that leads into a cozy room with laundry piled on the bed and stacks of books on the nightstands.

"And this"—she flings open the last door—"is my room."

Half the room is a Flor-nado, with a menagerie of stuffed animals and sparkly garments covering every surface. The other half is more controlled, with a loft bed over a desk cluttered with textbooks.

"Wow," I say. "That's a lot of stuffed animals."

Flor picks up a purple hippo. "This is Steve." Then a rainbow snake, a bright orange teddy bear, and possibly a gargoyle?—Hiss,

Boo, and Edward—and she would probably go on to name every single animal in the room if Maribel didn't come to rescue me.

"You can leave your stuff in here," she tells me. "But we'll go downstairs later. Come on, Chrysanthemum," she says to stave off Flor's impending tantrum over us not sleeping with her. "Dad says the pizza stuff is ready."

In the kitchen, a white man with graying brown hair stands behind the counter, wearing a flour-covered apron.

"Welcome to the finest pizza establishment in Shoreline," he says with a flourish. Flor giggles and Maribel looks like she wants to sink through the floor. "Grab a crust, pick your own toppings, and make some edible art!"

He drops his goofy performance face and smiles at me. "You must be Eden. I've heard a lot about you."

He holds out a floury hand to shake mine. "You can call me Paul."

"Nice to meet you."

I'm almost done putting my toppings on when a girl enters who looks exactly like Maribel's sister Soledad, if Soledad had a short, practical bob and wore nice jeans and a button-down shirt. (Which I can't imagine she ever would.)

"There's my girl." Their dad kisses the newcomer on the forehead and says, "Eden, this is Carmen. Carmen, Maribel's friend Eden."

"She's my friend," Flor insists, replacing a chunk of sausage that had rolled off her mountain of toppings.

"Hi, Eden." Carmen throws me a smile as she opens the refrigerator and pulls out a takeout container.

"Hey, what are you doing? We're making personal pizzas!" Paul says.

"Sorry, Dad, but my team's squeezing in one last practice tonight."

"You haven't achieved world peace yet?" he asks, shaking his head. "Come on, get it done."

"It was nice to meet you," Carmen says as she grabs keys off a hook by the door. "I can take the car, yeah?"

Paul waves a spatula at her, and she's gone as quickly as she came.

Flor insists on painting our toenails while the pizzas cook. Maribel's clearly annoyed, but I figure it's probably better to give Flor some attention now so she won't be so fussy later. Or maybe I'm making it worse by giving her attention. I don't know. I've never really hung around little kids.

"What color do you want?" Flor asks, opening up a fishing tackle box full of nail polish.

"Whoa. That is a lot of choices!"

Maribel rolls her eyes. "She's obsessed with nail polish. Last summer she hit the mother lode at the garage sale of a former manicurist."

"Sounds like you're the expert," I tell Flor. "You choose."

It's actually a perfect activity, because Flor is occupied, her brow scrunched in concentration as she paints my nails (and frankly a lot of my skin) a shocking grass green. This leaves Maribel and me free to talk.

"So are you going to Will's tomorrow? For Raven's sew-along?"

I jerk my foot away from Flor a little bit when she accidentally tickles me. "I really want to. I wish you were going to be there."

"Ugh, me too. Believe me, Carmen's Model UN competition is the last place I want to be. I am constantly being dragged to everyone's activities. What sucks is I don't really have anything they all have to go to. It's unfair."

"Fairness isn't everyone getting the same," Flor says, holding the nail polish wand up like she's making a decree. "Fairness is everyone getting what they need."

"Okay, Mom," Maribel grumbles. "I'm going to try out for the musical though," she says, eyes lighting up. "Maybe they'll all get dragged to that."

The whole house smells amazing by the time Paul calls us into the kitchen. Silvia is there, freshly showered, pouring glasses of wine for herself and Paul.

"Where are the big girls?" she asks as we sit down.

"Carmen's with her UN group," Paul says. "Soledad should be coming." He raises his wineglass to me. "But Eden's here!"

Paul makes polite conversation, asking about what my parents do, and what I think about volunteering at Casa Esperanza, and if I have any siblings. "Only child solidarity," he says, holding out his fist for a bump. "These girls have no idea how lucky they are to have a house full of sisters."

"Yeah," Maribel says. "Tell me that again when Sol and Carmen are hogging the bathroom on a school morning."

Flor shrugs. "I just pee outside."

Silvia drops her pizza onto her plate. "Flor!"

"What? No one can see me behind the hydrangea."

Before anyone can react to this, Soledad arrives in a rush. "Sorry, sorry I'm late," she says, planting kisses on both her parents' heads. "Hi, Eden. Nice to see you again."

"I made you a veggie pizza," her dad says. "It's keeping warm in the oven."

"Thanks, Dad." Soledad opens the oven and takes a deep inhale of the home-baked crust.

"What kept you from being home in time for family dinner?" Silvia asks.

"It's, like, the law," Maribel whispers to me, though obviously everyone can hear. "We have to be home for family dinner unless there's a preapproved reason. Except for Carmen, who apparently has her own rules."

"No lie," Soledad mutters as she slips into the empty seat across from me.

Silvia narrows her eyes. "Carmen has a very busy schedule of activities that are going to get her college scholarships."

Heading off an argument, Paul changes the subject. "What were you up to this afternoon, Sol?"

"There was a protest at City Hall about the Tigris tax."

Silvia nods, approving this reason for being late to dinner.

"What's the Tigris tax?" I ask.

All eyes turn to me. Everyone my age or older looks like they're considering how to explain it. Flor beats them to it: "Capitalist monsters want people to die on the streets."

Silvia chokes on her bite of pizza at the same time that Paul snorts a swallow of his wine.

"She's not wrong," Soledad says.

"It's a little more complex than that," Silvia amends.

"Basically, Tigris is this massive company based in Seattle," Maribel begins. I obviously know that—everyone knows Tigris—

but I'm starting to see that Maribel feels a little overshadowed in her family, so I keep my mouth shut. "And they've brought lots of jobs to the city—"

"You mean they've shuttered countless small businesses," Soledad says.

"Let her finish." Paul helps himself to some salad.

"But yeah, mostly they've had some really bad effects on the city: big increases in traffic, shutting down small businesses, and driving housing costs up, all while they make massive amounts of money."

They all nod like they talk about this stuff every night. Even four-year-old Flor knows more than I do! I'm kind of embarrassed to ask, but it's that or feel even more in the dark. "But what's the tax part?"

"Well, last fall a group of concerned citizens proposed a tax," Soledad takes over, oblivious to Maribel's scowl. "A tiny tax on Tigris, the money from which would be used to help Seattle's horrific homelessness problem."

"That's a really good idea."

"Isn't it? Except the Seattle City Council just decided against it. They're too afraid of making Tigris mad and losing all the business they bring to the city if Tigris picked up and left."

"We'd be better off," Silvia says, putting some salad on Flor's plate.

"So that's what you were protesting?"

"Yeah," Soledad says. "A lot of good it will do."

"It's always good to make your voice heard," Silvia says.

After dinner and several rounds of Candy Land with Flor, Maribel and I take my stuff and some blankets down to the basement. I was envisioning something dark and dreary, but it's a bright open space, with doors out to the backyard, and two very comfy looking couches and a massive beanbag.

"This is so cool."

"I keep trying to convince my parents to let me make it my bedroom," Maribel says. "But they say we need the space for family time."

It makes sense. Her family is big and the upstairs living room is cramped. Down here, there's room for everyone to have movie marathons and game nights and charades, and whatever else big happy families do.

"I'm hoping when Sol moves out, I can at least room with Carmen instead of Flor. But Carmen's not exactly onboard with that." She flops dramatically onto one of the couches. "You're so lucky you have your own room! And a dog!"

And she's so lucky to have parents who are around and involved, sisters to talk to and play with and even fight with. But the grass is always greener, I guess.

I always had a natural talent for the uneven bars. I was instantly comfortable from the first time I got up there, while floor exercise was the bane of my existence. I wanted to set my own rhythm, rather than have it dictated by the music. Meanwhile, my teammate Russell was the queen of the floor, forever griping that she wished she had my confidence on the bars.

So I guess this is normal, wanting what you don't have. But I can't help but feel like what I want—supportive family and connection—is a little bit more important than having a bigger room.

In the morning the family is up and moving early, since Carmen has to be in Bellingham for the Model UN competition at ten, and everyone is going along to cheer her on (whether they like it or not).

"Are you sure you don't want to come with us?" Maribel asks hopefully as we pile into the minivan.

The plan is for them to drop me at home on their way out of town. Later, Mom will (hopefully) take me to Raven and Will's.

"Maybe next time," I say.

"You're going to the sew-along, right?" Silvia says from the driver's seat.

"I think so."

"You should," Soledad says as she somehow manages to paint on a perfect cat eye in a moving car. "Raven's crew is the best."

"Do you sew?" Soledad's style is so cool, and it would be even cooler if I knew she made the clothes herself.

But she laughs as she moves on to lining her lips. "No, I'm hopeless. But I go to the sew-alongs when I can because the people are amazing. Raven's friend Preeti is the one who got me involved in fighting Initiative One Eighty-Two."

"The Tigris tax," Maribel supplies at my questioning look.

"Oh, wow." That's cool for Soledad, but somehow it makes me even more nervous to show up at this place where I barely know anybody, to do a thing I barely know how to do, and now I learn that they're political activists about stuff I know nothing about?

Too bad there aren't any pressing gymnastics issues in front of the Washington State legislature.

The whole time we're talking, Carmen is sitting in the very

back with earbuds in and head down in a massive notebook. Flor's also surprisingly quiet, slumped in her car seat, holding on to a stuffed caterpillar.

"Is she okay?" I ask Maribel.

Maribel nods. "She has bad nightmares sometimes. When she's had a rough night, it takes her a long time to wake up in the morning."

I used to have a lot of nightmares too. When I was really little, we lived in a small apartment and I'd go across the hall and climb into my mom's bed. But as MySecret took off and we moved into our current house, something shifted. My mom never said I couldn't come into her room anymore. But it was all the way at the end of a long hall, and making that trek in the middle of the night when I was already scared was too much.

So I suffered alone.

I'm glad Flor has Maribel in the same room with her, even if Maribel isn't.

"Who are these people again?" Mom asks as we follow the car's navigation to Raven and Will's house.

"Raven's Silvia's best friend," I explain again. "And Maribel is really close to her son, Will."

"And they invited you over to sew?"

"It's a sew-along. Making cloth pads."

Mom purses her lips and says nothing.

Raven and Will's house turns out to be an apartment in Mountlake Terrace. Mom walks me up to the building, where the ancient buzzer system doesn't seem to work.

"It's okay," I say, pulling out my phone. "I can text Raven."

A minute later Will is there, pushing open the door, red faced and out of breath like he ran to come let me in.

"Oh, hello," he says politely. "I'm Will."

"Hello, Will." Mom turns to me. "Do you want me to come in with you?"

"No, I'm good."

She pauses and then nods. "All right, then. Text me when you want me to pick you up." She turns to go and then turns back. "Have a good time."

Will's apartment is on the ground floor at the back of the building. "My mom manages the building," he explains, when I see the plaque by their front door with Raven's name and phone number on it.

If my house and Maribel's are different worlds, Will's apartment is a different planet. The walls are covered with artwork in vivid styles, interspersed with photos of Raven and Will, most of which look like they were taken on travels to interesting places. Every surface is covered too—candles and knickknacks and interesting carvings and sculptures.

Will leads me down a short hallway and through a curtain of hanging beads and bells, into a combo living room/dining room, where Raven holds court at the dining table, which is covered with fabric and three sewing machines.

"Eden!" She beams, like I'm some important guest and the real work can begin now that I've arrived. "I'm so glad you're here. Are you open to hugs?"

I blink at the question. I'm not sure anyone's ever asked me before. I nod, and suddenly Raven's arms are wrapped around me, along with her scent of herbs and essential oils and I don't know what all. Basically, she smells like the natural foods store (in a good way).

Will drifts off to the kitchen as Raven makes the rounds introducing me to the people stationed around the room.

Vincent's an older Black man sitting on the floor of the living room, operating this metal contraption that squeezes the edges of the pads, which then emerge with a snap pressed firmly in. He nods regally at me and carries on with his work.

LuAnn is also on the floor, cutting fabric. She's around Raven's age, white, with pure white hair in long braids. "Hey, Eden," she says. "I hear you're a sewing prodigy!"

My cheeks flush. "I don't know about that."

Preeti and Samira are a South Asian mother and daughter, and they're operating two of the sewing machines but pause to say hello and welcome me.

Raven returns to her spot behind the third sewing machine as Will returns with a bottle of something that looks like fruit juice.

"Kombucha?"

I've heard of it, but I've never tasted it. I take the bottle as Will proudly says, "My mom makes it herself."

I don't want to be rude, but I can't stop the face I make when the fizzy sour flavor explodes on my taste buds.

Samira laughs. "Kombucha is an acquired taste, for sure."

Raven's not offended at all. In fact, she's grinning. "You can leave it here," she says. "I'll finish it. Will, maybe some water instead?"

Will gives me a brief tour of the apartment, which doesn't take long. His bedroom has posters of the Sounders and the Reign, along with a signed Megan Rapinoe jersey on the wall.

"Soccer fan?"

"Yeah." He grins. "I'm not the best player. But I try! Have you ever been to a Sounders game?"

I went once with my mom, but we were in a fancy box where everyone was drinking champagne and eating caviar and not even paying attention to the game. I envision Will in the regular seats, face painted green and blue, shouting into the rain, and I'm pretty sure my version of a Sounders game doesn't count.

"Nope."

"You should, if you get the chance. Even if you're not a soccer fan. I dare you to resist the excitement."

He trips over a duffel bag on his way to a terrarium, where he reaches in to pet something. I hang back, a little afraid of what's in there. "Is that . . . a snake?"

"Bearded dragon!" He pulls out a sleepy-looking lizard-thing the size of his forearm. "This is Fyrian."

"Wow."

"No pressure, but he's super chill. He'll only bite if you're a roach." He holds out his arms, his reptile friend draped across them.

I approach slowly and the bearded dragon doesn't seem to notice I'm there. I don't want to go anywhere near the head, but I tentatively run a finger down his tail. It's scratchy. "What's his name again?"

"Fyrian," Will says, putting him back in the enclosure. "Have you read *The Girl Who Drank the Moon*?"

"Oh yeah . . . the tiny dragon?"

"Who believes he's huge! Yeah. I love that book. Sometimes who we are inside doesn't match who we are outside."

"There she is, the sewing prodigy!" Raven announces when we return to the group. She moves to give me her spot at the machine.

"Oh no," I say. "I'll do something easy." I look around the room at the options. I don't know how to use the snap machine. Cutting fabric looks like a pretty precise operation. Maybe I could pack up boxes of finished pads?

"Nonsense," Raven says. "You've got a machine at home, right? So let's get you really comfortable here, and then you'll be set to make more on your own. If you want."

"I do want to." I take Raven's spot, and she hands me some already-cut pieces of fabric.

"You want to line up the edges. When you're getting started, it can help to pin them together before you begin. Once you're an old pro, in about a week or so, you probably won't need to."

I grope around for the latch that lowers the presser foot, sandwiching the pieces of fabric together tight, and then step on the pedal that makes the machine go.

"Don't forget to backstitch," Will says from across the table, where he's started to pin together more layers of cut fabric.

"You sew too?" I ask.

"Oh yeah. Will's made more than I have, I think," Raven says.

Will grins and wiggles his fingers at me. "What can I say? I've got magic fingers!"

Raven chuckles. "Honestly, it's a miracle he hasn't sewn those fingers together."

I make my way slowly around the edges of the pad, picking up speed as I gain confidence.

"Whoa, hang on there—"

I've gone all the way around and veered off the fabric. My cheeks burn. This was a stupid idea.

"It's fine," Raven says. "You just have to leave a couple of inches unsewn, so we can turn it inside out."

I'm mortified, like I've fallen on my butt in the middle of a floor routine. Except in that situation, I'd know how to get back up and keep going, convincing the judges and audience nothing went wrong. But I can't fix this. I've wasted this fabric, and while my mom has bins of it, they probably have to use it carefully—

"No big deal." Raven retrieves the fabric from the machine and picks up a tiny pair of scissors. "We just rip the seam open like this. . . ." She undoes an inch of stitching and then turns it inside out. "Voilà. Now you try again."

She wants me to keep going? "No, I don't want to mess up again. I'll just . . . I could run out and buy some coffees?"

Raven studies me, puzzled. "Eden, of course you're going to mess up. That's why I invited you—so you can learn. But you learn by messing up. So try again." She hands me another set of cut-out fabric.

Learning by messing up is one thing, but there's a room full of people watching. Desperate to get it right, I go through the steps slowly and carefully. Partway through, Raven puts a hand on my shoulder. I freeze. "Honey, breathe," she says. "This should be fun. If it's not fun, then we can definitely find something else for you to do."

I take a deep breath and finish the pad. I even backstitch without being reminded, and then pull the sewn pad from the machine.

"Nice," Will says. "Trade you." He hands me the pieces he's pinned together and takes the ones I've just sewn, turning them right side out through the gap I left.

"How many have you made?" I ask.

"Me, personally?" He laughs. "I don't know. Thousands?"

"Whoa. You've helped so many women!"

A cloud passes over Will's face.

"Not only women," Raven says lightly.

"Oh." I'm not sure what I'm missing. "I mean, girls, too."

"We try to use the term 'menstruators.'" Raven squeezes Will's shoulder. I'm definitely missing something.

"I made the same mistake," Preeti says, stopping her own machine. "I was stuck in my ways and didn't realize there are boys who menstruate too."

Boys who menstruate too? It's another moment like Maribel's dinner table, where everyone else knew about the Tigris tax and I was struggling to catch up. Will's watching me carefully, like whatever I say next matters a whole lot. He gives the tiniest smile and a shy little wave, and fifth-grade sex ed—dividing us into girls and boys—suddenly collides with the reality in front of me. *Sometimes who we are inside doesn't match who we are outside.*

Heat crawls up my cheeks as I realize Will's not the only one watching me. "I'm so sorry," I say. "I didn't realize."

"That's cool," Will says.

But I'm not sure if it is.

"Seriously," Skye adds, holding up her hand for a high five.

"Really?"

"Are you kidding?" Julie leans in, lowering her voice. "I was one ' the first in my class to get my period, in the beginning of sixth ade. I bled through my gym shorts, and Graham has never let ' forget it!"

"We have to wear white shorts for lacrosse, and whoever ned that uniform obviously doesn't get periods."

Ion't know if Skye and Julie are friendlier than the girls sit with, or if it's that I suddenly have something to ' iat isn't gymnastics, but we spend the rest of lunch in on- atter. Julie walks with me as we both head towa asses st wing.

I pull out my phone to see if Dad ha ded yet, she nd punches her number in, then grins d ducks into the in before I can say anything in resp se.

anza is abuzz with activity n Maribel and I arrive g Suspension may be up, that's no reason for me an empty house. Si Raven, and Barbara are an informational ting about a proposed tent stal ss people in the ighborhood. Lots of neighbors tha ried that crim will go up if homeless people are beinc e here.

ecor live here," ilvia cries. "Sorry, sorry. I know I'm th hoir."

he lo ops up when s ees us from where she was sit- mp oor, aying with tru "Come play! You can be the k. It y best one."

Maribel's about to object, but I squat down to vroom the truck around for a minute while Raven sums up the meeting.

"Basically," she says, "it's not a done deal. The city council should make their decision in the next few days."

"How will it affect Casa Esperanza?" I ask.

Silvia smiles. "That's a really good question, Eden. I think our services will be more necessary than ever. While it's true there are already plenty of unhoused people living in Shoreline, a tent city a few blocks from here would mean more people needing services in a concentrated area. We would definitely need to do some big supply drives to keep up."

"Meanwhile, Tigris builds a massive new distribution center up the road," Barbara says, her brow knitting with quiet fury.

"Seriously, the tiniest tax on them could house every unhoused person in Shoreline."

"In Seattle," Silvia adds.

"Honestly, the entire Pacific Northwest."

They're interrupted by a food bank volunteer calling that she needs help up front. Silvia and Barbara head out to help her, and Raven starts packing up her things.

"How's the sewing going, Eden?" she asks. "Make any more pads?"

"Not yet. My mom was using the machine on Sunday. But I'm going to!"

"That's so great," Raven says. "Truly, any questions you have—"

Maribel hands Raven the water bottle she was about to leave on the table. "Didn't you say you had to get Will to his soccer practice?"

"Why, yes, yes I did." Raven chuckles. "Look at you, all on top of everyone else's schedules. I wonder where you get that. . . ."

"Ugh!" Maribel says when Raven's gone. "I am nothing like my mom!"

"What are you talking about? Your mom is the best." If Silvia were my mom, I'd take that as a huge compliment. But I can understand not wanting other people to compare you to your mom. When I was competing, people were always telling me how I obviously had my mom's work ethic, or telling her no wonder her daughter was so driven. Mom ate it up. And it was kind of true. But was it true because I'm truly like her, or because I wanted to meet her sky-high expectations?

Flor waves a blue truck she's tied a sparkly ribbon around. "Eden's right," she announces.

Maribel rolls her eyes. "Of course she is."

"Thanks, Chrysanthemum," I say, grinning at Flor.

"You're just like Mami," she goes on to say. "You're both bossy."

I fight back a laugh, but then Maribel reaches out to grab Flor and tickle her, so I let it out. When she's had her payback, Maribel says very seriously to Flor, "You know we don't use the word 'bossy.'"

Flor looks down at the nubby carpet. "I know."

"What do we say instead?"

Flor sighs, then says as clearly as she can wrap her mouth around such big words: "Executive leadership skills."

"Yeah," I say as Flor runs out of the room to follow after Silvia, "you are a lot like your mom."

"Shush." Maribel yanks a notebook from her backpack. "New

topic." She pulls a flyer from her notebook and slides it across the table at me.

"Oh yeah, the musical? I saw your name on the sign-up sheet. That's so cool."

"Cool enough for you to audition?"

Oh, Eden. Good thing gymnasts don't need to sing.

I push it back at her. "No. No way. I am not a performance person."

"What are you talking about? Hello, elite gymnast?"

"That is not the same!"

"Really? Did you put on a costume and makeup?"

"Yeah, but—"

"Did you learn choreography and practice a bunch and get feedback and improve until you were ready to do it in front of an audience?"

"Judges, not an audience."

"Judges *and* an audience."

"Yes, fine. Maybe there are some similarities with floor exercise and, like, a dance performance, but floor was always my worst event! And I don't sing or act or any of that!"

"But don't you think it would be kind of fun? Just to be a small part. Like, third tree from the left?"

What do you do for fun?

"Are there even trees in *Joseph and the Amazing Technicolor Dreamcoat?*"

"I don't know, palm trees? Julie's done a bunch of shows with this director. She says she's totally amazing and fun, and we should do it!"

I'm annoyed with Maribel pushing me, but also annoyed because she's right that it sounds like fun, but also annoyed with myself because I know I'll never let myself try something I'm likely to flop at.

"I bet you'll be great," I finally say. I mean, I have no way of knowing if Maribel can act or sing, but she's confident and has a big personality, and that seems like half the battle.

"I thought it would be fun to do together," Maribel says, her enthusiasm dampened.

"It's not that I don't want to do it with you," I say, trying to soften the blow. The last thing I want to do is push away Maribel, my first post-gymnastics friend. "That part would be fun. . . ."

"Really! Oh, thank Frank!" She jumps out of her seat and starts pacing. "Okay, we have to pick songs, and then we can practice them together. Maybe after school tomorrow we can go back to my house instead of coming here. I might be able to convince Sol to drive us. . . ."

And just like that, I have lost her to planning auditions I didn't even agree to.

Chapter Ten

Maribel's house after school is just as bustling as Casa Esperanza. The moment we step in the door, Flor's asking me to play. Carmen and a group of friends are spread around the coffee table in the living room, working on a group project. Sol beelines for her room, and Paul offers us yogurt when we walk into the kitchen.

"No thanks, that would clog up our throats." Maribel grabs glasses of water for both of us and leads the way to her room.

"Thanks, anyway," I say to Paul as I follow Maribel.

Flor, wisely, ran to stake out her spot on her bed during our detour to the kitchen. It is her room too, after all. Maribel can't really kick her out, can she?

"Out," Maribel demands, holding the door open.

Apparently she can.

But Flor won't be gotten rid of that easily. She crosses her arms firmly across her chest. "No. This is my room too."

"Come on, Fl-Chrysanthemum."

Flor stares back at her sister flatly. She is unmoved by the use of her preferred name.

"We'll play with you after. Right now we need time to work on our auditions. In private."

Flor's resolve is impressive. Her expression never changes and she doesn't move a muscle.

"Dad!" Maribel howls.

A moment later Paul appears in the doorway. "Anyone bleeding?" he asks cheerfully. "Any major developmental milestones? No? Then work it out, my girls."

And then he's gone.

"Ugh!" Maribel fumes as Flor sits back smugly, folding her arms behind her head like she's settling in for a good, long while. "Fine," Maribel says. "Ignore her." She pulls a spiral notebook from her backpack and opens it to a page covered in writing, most of it scratched out. "I've been brainstorming audition songs. I've decided on 'Popular' for me." At my blank look, she adds, "It's Glinda's best song?"

I shrug. I don't remember a song called "Popular" from *The Wizard of Oz*, but I'm sure Maribel knows what she's doing.

"Oh boy," she mutters. "But for you, I wasn't sure what your range is."

"My range?"

"Your singing range? Like, soprano, alto?"

"I told you, I'm not a singer."

"Okay, don't worry about it. We'll experiment. I think "My Grand Plan" from *The Lightning Thief* could be really fun. It'll show your confidence."

"The Lightning Thief, like Percy Jackson?" I didn't even know it was a musical, but at least I've read the book.

"Yeah, it's Annabeth's song!" Maribel opens an ancient Chromebook and turns it on, but before she can show me a video, Flor explodes, unable to remain silent another second.

"'My grand plan,'" she belts, standing on her bed and spreading her arms wide, "'is that I will be remembered!'"

Maribel spins around in her desk chair, eyes blazing. Flor snaps her mouth shut. "One more peep," Maribel warns her, "and you are out of here."

She turns back to her computer and hits play. The song is catchy, about a girl who wants to go on quests and prove herself, but she's being held back. This girl's ambition, though—it gets under my skin. It's great to want big things, but planning for them just leads to disappointment. Too many things can happen that you didn't plan for, like torn labrums. I'm sure Maribel didn't even think about what the song would mean to me, someone who had to give up on her dreams. But somehow that annoys me even more.

"Catchy song," I manage. "But it's not really me."

"Are you kidding? You were going to the Olympics! You're all about ambition!"

That's not even true, though. People assume that if you're doing elite gymnastics at thirteen, you're definitely going to the Olympics, but only a tiny, tiny fraction of the people on my level end up competing on the national stage.

"Oh my gosh!" Maribel grabs my hands. "You were going to be an Olympian! An *Olympian*! Get it?"

Flor can't hold it in any longer. "Like Annabeth and Percy are

Olympians! In Percy Jackson! Or at least half! Their parents are gods! Annabeth's mother is Athena, the goddess of—"

"Out." There's fire in Maribel's eyes as she turns on Flor, and this time Flor can see she's gone too far.

"Fine," she says. "Don't blame me when you don't get into the play." And she stomps out of the room.

Maribel rolls her eyes, then turns her focus back to me. "Just trust me. This is your song."

"No." My voice comes out harsher than I mean it to, but being subtle doesn't seem to work on Maribel. "I'm not doing it! Would you stop pushing?"

She's shocked, like she's never been told no before. Except she has. She gets told no all the time in her big, busy family.

"Sorry for wanting to do something fun together." She turns away from me, busying herself with something on her desk.

I don't know what I'm supposed to do now. When I had problems with friends at the gym, I could just throw myself into training, or walk out of the locker room. What do I do here, go play with Flor?

It's not that I don't want to be friends with Maribel. Not at all. I just need to make my own choices for a change.

"Look, I'm sorry," I say. "About hurting your feelings. I've just been doing things because someone else told me to for a long time. So maybe I overreacted."

She turns back to me, looking hopeful.

"I still don't think it's right for me," I say, "but can you show me your song?"

Her eyes light up. She pulls up another video, but instead of sitting and watching it with me, she jumps up and strikes a pose in between the two beds. She launches into the song, and she not only knows the words but she's got moves and comedic head tilts, and honestly, she seems ready for the audition already.

"Wow," I say when the song ends. "That was amazing! Have you done a lot of theater before?"

She beams at my praise, but her face falls a little at the question. "No. I wish. We've never been able to afford the shows at theaters that you have to pay to be in. I did the talent show at Salmon Springs, and I've done some solos at my church. But my friend Macy was super into theater, and we used to make up choreography and routines all the time."

The way she says "was" makes me wonder if Macy died or something. "That sounds fun."

Maribel hands me one of those photo-booth strips of pictures of herself and a white girl with an explosion of curls, goofing around. "This is Macy," she says. "She had to move to Florida when her parents got divorced last summer."

Oh. That helps explain why bubbly, friendly Maribel seemed kind of adrift, friend-wise, at school.

"We were so excited that the middle school had a theater program," she says. "I guess that's why I was pushy about auditioning. Sorry."

Relief washes over me. "Oh my gosh, it's totally okay. Maybe I could do something behind the scenes."

She jumps off the bed. "Yes! Costumes! You're, like, a sewing wizard, right?"

I laugh. "I don't know about that."

Since we no longer have to worry about my audition, we return to Maribel's. She wants my critique, so I think about some of the language my coaches used when polishing my floor routines.

"I think you could be a little crisper with the movements," I say. "Like when you tilt your head after 'That's what makes me so nice,' it's super funny, but it would be even funnier if it was kind of sharp."

I demonstrate, and she tries it. I'm not wrong! It's even better.

Maribel is running through it again, hitting the funniest part of the song when there's a knock on the door. She scowls and flings it open to reveal not Flor but Will.

"Hey," he says. "Were you singing?"

"Oh! Hey!" Maribel tugs him in, peeks out into the hallway to make sure Flor isn't lurking, and then shuts the door behind him. "We're working on my audition. Want to see?"

Will sits on Flor's bed next to me, nodding for Maribel to do her thing. He laughs especially hard when she makes the sharp head tilt where I suggested it, which feels really good. Maybe that's what my coaches felt like when I nailed something.

"That was great," he says when she's done. "*Wicked*, right?" he turns to me. "Are you auditioning too, Eden?"

"Eden's got stage fright," Maribel says, which isn't strictly true, but whatever. "But you could audition, Will. Last year there was a homeschooled girl in *Grease!*"

He smiles at me. "I think I might have stage fright too. Plus, I'm pretty busy helping my mom prepare for the Guatemala trip. We're working on our Spanish. Mom's pretty good already, plus a couple of her local contacts speak good English."

"Is your mom going?" I ask Maribel.

"Nope, she's too busy saving the world here. Can I go through the song one more time for you guys? I feel like my timing was a little off in the last chorus."

"Go for it." Will sits back on the bed and his leg brushes against mine the littlest bit. Which is not a big deal. I just notice. Whatever.

Maribel finishes, having performed the piece perfectly again, but we clap and rave and she gulps down her water like she's run a marathon.

"Okay, I need some more water," she says. "Do you two want anything from the kitchen?"

We shake our heads and she leaves.

"How long have you known Maribel?" I ask after a couple of moments of silence.

"Our moms were in a childbirth preparation class together," he says. "So, our whole lives."

"Wow. I haven't known anyone that long. I mean, except family."

"My mom is the only family I have," Will says, but he doesn't sound sad about it. Just matter-of-fact.

"What about your dad?" I ask.

Will shrugs. "He's not really involved. We go visit, but that's about it."

But I think of the people at their apartment for the sew-along, and how they come and go from Casa Esperanza and Maribel's house like it's their own. "It seems like you've made a family, though."

He nods. "Yeah. My mom makes everyone she meets into family."

Silence falls again for a minute, and I can't help but notice Will smells like his mom a little, like incense and herbs, but also sort of

Christmassy, like pine trees and smoke or something. Why am I noticing how he smells?

"Your mom actually gave me an idea," I blurt.

"Oh yeah?"

"Yeah, she was at Casa Esperanza yesterday and she said a tiny tax on Tigris could house all the unhoused people in the Pacific Northwest."

"That sounds like her," Will says. "But my mom and her friends have been fighting Tigris for years. They never get anywhere. It's way too powerful."

Which is exactly what I was thinking. Tigris is more than a big company. It's a behemoth. And housing all the unhoused people in the Pacific Northwest is also an incredibly massive, unwieldy goal.

But what if the goal were more manageable?

"Okay, but what if . . . ," I say slowly, shocked that the first person I'm telling this idea to is a boy, but he is a boy who helped me learn to sew pads, so here we go. "What if a tax on a big company—I'm not talking mammoth like Tigris, but big companies like my mom's—what if a tax on big companies in Seattle could supply free menstrual products for people who need them?"

Will's eyebrows shoot up.

"Never mind, it's probably dumb."

"No, it's amazing. So, wait, let's be more specific. Free for whoever needs them is pretty broad."

"Okay, well schools would be a good start."

"That's perfect! A law was passed in 2021 that requires schools and universities to provide free menstrual products."

"Oh." I think back to the empty machine in my school's bathroom. "I'm not sure that's always enforced."

"No, it's not!" Will shifts so he's sitting cross-legged, facing me. "That's because the law says schools have to have them, but the state doesn't give the schools the money to do it."

"Well, that's dumb! How are they supposed to follow the law, then?"

"Exactly! Maybe by a tax like you're suggesting! And also, the law says they have to be provided in gender-neutral bathrooms too, but how many schools even have those?"

"Not mine."

"Plus, there are lots of places besides schools that could have supplies. Like any public bathroom? Libraries? Parks? Homeless shelters?"

"Yes!"

Maribel returns with her glass of water and a bowl of grapes. "What are we talking about?"

"Eden has this really cool idea for an initiative," Will says.

"A what?" I ask.

"An initiative! It's how you get a law on the ballot. Anyone can propose one."

"Nooo!" Maribel sinks down on the floor, head in hands. "It's already all politics all the time around here! I need a break, I beg of you!"

"No, but this is seriously cool," Will says. "Listen—"

Before he can explain, my phone rings and my mom's face appears on the screen. She never calls, so I answer right away.

"Mom?"

"Eden? Good, are you home?"

"No, I'm at Maribel's, remember? You're supposed to pick me up at six."

"Right. Well. Can you call a car? I just got a call from Mrs. Bloom."

"Who?"

"Mrs. Bloom! The lady on the corner? Apparently Blizz got out and has been rampaging through her roses. She chased after him, which only drove him farther down the street."

My stomach turns over. How did Blizz get out? How far has he gotten? What if he gets hit by a car or falls down a ravine or—

"Eden, are you listening? I have an extremely important call with our European distributor this evening. There is no way I can leave. Can you call a car?"

"I guess?"

"Okay, hon, I'm going to trust you've got this covered. I've got to go."

The call clicks off and I'm left with the phone in my hand, tears springing to my eyes as I open the RydeKids app.

"What's wrong?" Maribel asks as Will looks on in concern.

I explain the situation while I search for the nearest ride. Twelve minutes before they'd even get here. As soon as she hears that, Maribel is out the door. Will and I follow her to the living room, where she's catching Silvia and Raven up on the situation.

"So can we take her home?" Maribel asks her mom.

Silvia looks stricken. "Your dad took Flor to ballet and Carmen left with my car."

"But we have to help her!" Maribel shrieks. "We can't wait twelve minutes!"

Raven stands, calm as ever. "Hey, hang on. Will and I can take her. We were about done here anyway."

"I don't understand," Maribel says, trailing me out to Raven's colorful van. "How did he get out? You have a fully fenced yard, right?"

"Yeah. And he stays inside when no one's home anyway."

"Doggie door?"

"No."

"Don't worry, Mar," Will says, opening the door for me. "We'll find him."

As we climb in, Maribel walks away and I swear I hear her mutter, "Maybe some people shouldn't have dogs if they aren't going to take care of them. . . ."

Will winces. "Look, Maribel's kind of black and white. If she's your friend, she's your best friend for life. But if you cross her, there are going to be big feelings."

"How did I cross her?"

"You didn't. It's just . . . she's obsessed with dogs. But can't ever have one. Look, it's going to be fine."

Raven climbs into the driver's seat. "All will be well! In college, the girl across the hall from me had a pet snake, and of course we weren't supposed to have pets, and it escaped. We had to search the six-story building, and I'm the one who found it!"

I shudder.

"Where was it?" Will asks.

"In the laundry room! All curled up in a pile of warm laundry!"

It makes sense that a snake would go somewhere warm. But where would Blizz go, outside of our yard? He only ever goes on leashed walks with me. It's not like he knows any neighbors. You read those stories about dogs that make cross-country trips to make their way back to their real homes. But Blizz's only other home was a breeder in Vancouver.

"Hey, Mom," Will says. "Remember when you worked on that ballot initiative with Preeti? How did that work again?"

Raven starts an explanation that has to do with getting signatures on a petition, but I'm too focused on Blizz, and on what Maribel said.

She's not wrong that I never really wanted a dog. I'm sure she'd make a much better dog owner than I am. But whether I wanted the adorable fluff ball or not, I have him. He's my responsibility. And somehow he escaped, which was probably my fault.

"I know I'm headed to Richmond Highlands," Raven says from the front seat. "But you're going to need to give me specifics."

"Oh right, sorry. Go west on One Seventy-Fifth."

"Can anyone start a petition for an initiative?" Will asks.

"Any registered voter," Raven says.

"So they have to be eighteen?"

"Yep."

"You turn left up here, after that old-timey light post," I say. "And we're close now, so look out for a small white dog."

Will drops all questions about petitions and initiatives and glues his face to the car window.

"That Japanese maple," I point out. "That's our driveway."

Raven pulls into our massive driveway in front of our massive house, and I want to disappear, thinking of their modest apartment full of love and friends and warmth.

"So," Will says, "is Blizz a small, fluffy white dog with a blingy turquoise collar?"

I follow his gaze to see Blizz. Curled up on the front doormat.

"Blizz!"

I launch myself out of the car, run, and throw myself down on the front step, gathering Blizz's wiggly, warm body into my arms.

"Hey," Will says, "he's okay. Everything's okay."

It takes me a minute to realize I'm crying. In front of Will, and Raven, who's climbing out of her car now too. Will sits down next to me and scratches behind Blizz's ears. The little traitor immediately hops over onto Will's lap.

"That must have been scary." Raven crouches down into a yoga squat in front of me. "Pets can really be like family members."

"But he's not," I manage, my voice wobbly. "I take terrible care of him!"

Raven's quiet for a minute. "When Will was little—I mean really little—he got out of the apartment we were living in at the time, which was on the ground floor, and somehow made his way out of the building."

Will groans, but Raven goes on, undaunted. "I'd been in the shower for five minutes. Thought he was all settled watching *Sesame Street*. I only figured out what had happened because he left our door and the building door wide open."

"What happened?"

Will buries his face in Blizz's fur as Raven grins. "I found him two blocks down, sitting next to a dumpster and feeding a rat."

"Even as a toddler, he was better with animals than I am."

Raven frowns, then glances at the front door. "Is anyone home?"

"No, my mom's at work."

"Can we come in? I think our work here is not yet done."

I'm not sure what that means, and I'm definitely self-conscious about inviting them into our house, but I've already blubbered all over them. I don't have much else to lose.

"Sure." I unlock the door, and Blizz skitters around their feet as we make our way inside.

"Where's the kitchen?" Raven asks, seemingly oblivious to the rest of the house.

I lead the way and she starts opening cupboards as soon as we get there.

"Mom!" Will says.

"Oh, sorry, do you mind?" she asks.

I shrug. "Can I help you find something?"

She wrinkles her nose at the skim milk in the fridge. "Where would I find turmeric?"

I have no idea what that is. I turn to Will.

"It's a spice," he says in a stage whisper.

"Oh, yeah, no. We don't cook."

Raven sighs. "How about tea, then?"

Tea, we have! My mom buys all the fancy teas she sees on Instagram and I don't know where, which promise to detox or halt the aging process or heal the gut, like some dried-up leaves can even do that.

I point her to the cupboard, and Raven rummages through while I watch Blizz chase after a ball Will's tossing down the hallway.

"This'll work," she mutters, selecting a box with a picture of a serene lady meditating. She fills the teapot and puts water on to boil. Then she sits on a barstool and pats the one next to her.

"Honey," she says. "Animals get out. People make mistakes. So what's this really about?"

I kind of don't want Will to hear what an awful person I am, but somehow feel like I can tell Raven anything.

"I didn't want him," I admit. "Blizz. And I'm trying to take care of him anyway, but maybe I don't do the best job because I shouldn't have had him in the first place."

And maybe my mom always puts work first because she never planned on having a kid. I know she didn't. I read it in an interview with her once, where she was talking about having it all and work-life balance, and she said it's a myth, no one can have it all, and it's ridiculous that women are expected to. That women are judged harshly for putting work first, or worse, choosing not to have kids at all. And that life throws you curveballs and sometimes you end up on a path you didn't intend, but you still deserve to fight like hell for your dreams.

The teakettle screams, and Raven gets up to pour the water into two mugs.

"Your mom got him for you?" she asks.

"My dad. He loves dogs, and he's not around a lot because he's a pilot. . . ." I trail off. It sounds dumb when I say it out loud. Obviously, a dog isn't a substitute for a father. My dad doesn't even think that. "He really meant well."

"I'm sure he did." Raven places a cup of tea in front of me. "But if you're really not up for taking care of him, you shouldn't have to keep him. I think your dad would understand. Someone else would love to have him."

Like Maribel, I think.

"But on the other hand, maybe you just need more time, or help training him, or some kind of support. What do you think?"

I watch Will, who has somehow already taught Blizz to sit before he'll throw the ball for him again. I take a sip of the tea, which is sweeter than I expected, and soothing on my tight throat.

"Maybe."

At lunch the next day, Maribel chatters with Julie about the auditions. She barely glances my way. When Julie gets up to grab another fruit cup, I say, "Blizz was waiting on our doorstep when we got there."

She nods. "I know. Raven texted my mom."

"She's so great."

"Raven? Yeah. But don't get too attached, to her or Will. They're always leaving." There's an edge to Maribel's voice I've never heard before. I thought she was okay with me not auditioning, but she's obviously upset about something.

"Like the Guatemala trip?"

"Yeah, or off to Chicago for three months, or the summer before last they took an RV across the country. Like my mom says, 'Raven's a visionary, but she's not the most reliable.' Same goes for Will."

On this ominous declaration, Maribel turns back to Julie, who has returned with fruit cups for both of them.

I don't think Maribel's chilliness is about the audition anymore. It felt like we got through that yesterday. But something else happened between then and now. Is she seriously mad at me because Blizz got out?

After school, I'm waiting for a car, but then I get a text from Will.

Are you coming to CE today?

I wasn't. But the idea that I might see Will makes my stomach give a little flip.

I can. Why?

Come. I have a surprise for you.

I cancel the car and start walking toward Casa Esperanza instead. When I get there, Will flings the door open when I'm halfway across the parking lot. "Finally! Come in, come in!" He grabs my hand and tugs me through the food bank.

I wave to Barbara, who's restocking the grains section. She chuckles as I trip over a box of diapers in the aisle.

"Sorry!" I call, because Will is not going to let me stop and put it back where it goes. Did I mention he's holding my hand?

In the office, Silvia looks up, mildly startled.

"Maribel had auditions today," I remind her. "Will invited me."

"Of course," she says. "You're always welcome here, Eden."

Finally, Will tugs me into the classroom, where Soledad sits, studying. Will shuts the door, then throws his arms out, dramatically presenting Soledad as the surprise.

I put up a hand in a tentative wave. "Hi?"

"Oh, good, you're here. Come sit next to me." Soledad moves some papers out of the way and sets an iPad at the seat next to her.

I sit as she powers on the iPad and presents it to me.

"So these are the steps to proposing an initiative in Washington State. First, you have to be a registered voter."

I blink, then glance toward Will, who's grinning like he's given me the best birthday present ever. "I'm thirteen."

"Yes, but *I* am eighteen."

"Sol will propose the initiative for us!" Will blurts, unable to contain himself for another second.

"Are you sure?" A quick glance at the list of steps on the iPad in front of me tells me this is a complicated process.

"Of course," she says, with a wave of purple-and-green-striped fingernails. "I've been needing a senior project anyway, and this is perfect. Plus, you two are totally helping."

"And Maribel," I say.

They both look at me skeptically. "Doubt it," Soledad says. "So I've helped on an initiative before, but this is my first time as point person. But I'm pretty sure this is how it goes."

Soledad goes on to explain the process to us, which is basically this: First, we need to draft the text of the initiative, which is like an essay explaining what we're proposing, being as clear and detailed as possible. Then we set up an account with the Office of the Secretary of State, pay a five-dollar fee, and upload the text we drafted.

Once that's approved, we have to collect signatures on a petition to put our initiative on the ballot in the fall.

"Wait, so that's like the people who stand outside grocery stores with clipboards?"

"Exactly," Soledad says.

I cringe. I can't imagine asking strangers for a favor. "How many signatures do we need?"

"That's a little complicated. We need eight percent of the total number of votes cast in the last governor's election."

I'm starting to think this was a huge mistake. I am not a math person. But Will has his phone out already.

"In 2020, 4,116,894 voters. Which means we need . . . 329,351 signatures."

I gape at him. "How did you do that?"

He flashes his phone at me, showing me the calculator app. Still, I wouldn't have known how to do that so fast.

"That's a lot of signatures."

"It is. But that's statewide," Soledad says. "We could also propose it just for our county, which would be a lot fewer."

"But making it statewide would help a lot more people," Will points out. "Why limit ourselves?"

He's so excited. Soledad is too. She's subtler about it, but I can tell from the way she's tapping her fingers and the sparkle in her perfectly lined eyes.

Their excitement kindles something in me, too. It's familiar. It's being presented with a new gymnastics skill that seems impossible at first. But I never shut it down before I try. Like Will said, why limit ourselves?

"Okay," I say. "I'm in."

Chapter Eleven

That night Mom brings home Indian food at eight o'clock. I'd had a bowl of cereal around six, and I'm about to say so when she says, "Hang on, there's one more thing!"

She disappears back into the garage and returns lugging a massive box. She trips on one of Blizz's toys right inside the door and almost goes down, but I reach her in time to steady her and help her guide the box onto the kitchen table.

It's a Juki Sayaka sewing machine with, according to the box, 350 stitches, a touch-screen interface, and a buttonhole sensor system, whatever that is.

"But . . . we already have a sewing machine."

"Not like this one! This one is computerized, with a much bigger work space, and all sorts of presser feet included. It's got digital tension!"

I have no idea what that means, only that it's way more than I need to make pads.

"That old one is barely a step up from sewing by hand. This is going to be so much easier for you." She beams. Then she bustles away toward the stairs. "I'm going to change. Would you set up the food?"

I sigh. I'm supposed to be grateful. And I guess I am. But I didn't ask for this. I don't need it! Even if I end up doing the costumes for Maribel's show, the old machine worked fine. I'm already intimidated by the list of new features on the box as I haul it off the table to set out our plates.

That's when I see the price tag. Four thousand dollars?!

I'm still standing there in shock, the food still in its Styrofoam containers, when Mom waltzes back into the room in her cashmere loungewear.

"What are you doing?" she says. "I cooked, the least you could do is serve the food."

It's a joke we make, saying she cooked when she only picked up takeout, but I am not in the mood. "You didn't cook. You paid someone else to do the work," I snap.

She brushes past me to set the samosas on the table. "What's your problem?"

"My problem," I say, my voice wobbling, "is that I didn't ask for a brand-new sewing machine. Especially one that cost four thousand dollars!"

She sets chana masala down with enough force that some slops out onto the table. "Most people say thank you when they receive a nice gift they didn't even ask for."

"But I don't need it! The one we have works perfectly! And you don't even seem to realize it's an absurd amount of money!"

"Absurd amounts of money never bothered you when you needed competition leos or private coaching."

"Okay." I take a breath. I know I seem like an ungrateful brat. I know she works hard for our money, and that I have gotten tons of advantages because of it. "But think about how much money that is. Grandma could live on that for ages."

"You know how Grandma feels about me giving her money." Mom's eyes are blazing now. I have a feeling no one is going to eat that chana masala tonight.

"Okay, not Grandma. But four thousand dollars would buy . . . how many boxes of MySecret products for Casa Esperanza? Or you could supply all the homeless shelters in Seattle! You could pay someone's rent for . . . I don't know, at least a couple of months!"

"Fine, I get it," she snaps. "I'm a clueless fat cat CEO who has no idea what it's like to live in poverty. It's not like I grew up in it or anything!" She slams the last carton of Indian food on the table, then grabs a bottle of wine and stomps out of the kitchen.

The next morning the world's most expensive sewing machine is still on the table, along with the congealed Indian food. Mom's already gone.

As I wait for the car to arrive, I check my phone. I have texts from my dad, taking off in London and landing in New York; from Will, sharing advice he found online about the most effective ways to gather signatures; and one from Grandma that's a GIF of a panda rolling down a slide.

I respond to Dad and Grandma, saving Will for later. The whole sewing machine debacle last night sort of overshadowed the meeting with Will and Soledad and this exciting thing we're (maybe/probably?) embarking on.

It's a brand-new world, politics and activism. But Will and

Soledad know what they're doing. It's hard to be the beginner and let others be the leader. But the fact is, the one thing I was an expert on is no longer my thing. So I had to be a beginner at something eventually. It might as well be this thing that makes me feel like I want to go out and slay some dragons.

Mom will probably think I'm rebelling against her and the time she's spent on MySecret that she hasn't spent on me. But that isn't it. It's more that I'm finally seeing outside myself and realizing there are so many problems in the world and I can't solve them all. I mean, I can't solve any of them. But I can make a dent in one issue in my corner of the world.

Gymnastics was such an isolated world. Always about me and my body and my focus and my achievements. Sometimes it was my team, or my club. But mostly it was all focused inward, like the rest of the world didn't exist. I'd hear about things, like elections or natural disasters or whatever, and I'd know they were happening and I'd care, but I didn't have any extra energy to do anything.

Now I have nothing but energy, and finally somewhere to put it.

Skye's in my math class right before lunch, so we walk together to the cafeteria. She's usually the quietest one at our lunch table—though that's not hard with Maribel and Julie competing for the spotlight—but in math class, she's a whiz, answering every question. At one point Mr. Knabb had to step out of the room, and he asked Skye to explain interval notation.

"You're so good at math," I tell her as we navigate the crowded hallways. "I've never understood that before, but the way you explained it was so clear. You could be a teacher."

She shakes her head, the beads on the ends of her braids clicking together as she does. "Thanks, but I'm going to be a NASA engineer."

Whoa. She says it with so much certainty, I'm sure it's going to happen. I have more questions. But then we turn a corner to find a group of kids crowded around a bulletin board. Emerging from the group, Maribel and Julie are holding hands and jumping up and down, squealing.

The other kids are in varying states of reaction. One girl is crying, a couple are texting, looking disappointed, and some are high-fiving and chattering together. In some ways I can't relate to this world at all. But at the same time, it's not so different finding out who qualified for certain events.

When Julie and Maribel finally notice us standing there, they come running over.

"I got the Narrator!" Julie squeals.

Then they're jumping again. I turn to Maribel. "What about you?"

"I got Pharaoh." She grins. "It's not as big a part as Julie's, but she has way more experience. She totally deserves Narrator. And Pharaoh has a super fun song."

"The best song," Julie adds, linking her arm through Maribel's.

"This is going to be so much fun!" Maribel squeals. "We're taking over the drama department! Eden's going to make us fabulous costumes! And, Skye, you should do crew!"

She and Julie grab Skye and me, so we're linked into a tight little circle. "We'll all be in it together!"

Skye's happy for them, I can tell, but she shakes her head. "I'm really busy with lacrosse," she says. "But I'm totally coming to see the show."

Maribel's and Julie's faces fall for a second, but they quickly recover and return to celebrating. I'm pretty sure Skye and I will be quickly forgotten, but I'm surprised when Maribel turns and says, "You, come with me, now."

She marches me away from the other two.

"Where are we going?"

"To see Dot!"

She marches me to the drama room. It's lined on one side with mirrors, like where we'd practice choreo at the gym. Rows of chairs are arranged on risers to one side with a nearby piano, and stacks of blue mats line the other wall.

A stab of something like homesickness passes through me at the sight of those grimy blue mats.

Maribel pulls me across the room to a door into the smallest office I've ever seen. I'm fairly certain it was meant to be a closet, but a desk has been wedged inside and the walls are lined with framed production photos. A small woman with spiky gray hair and the most outrageous rainbow eyeglasses I've ever seen sits behind the desk.

"Well, if it isn't my Pharaoh," she says with a broad smile. "Congratulations, Maribel. I'm thrilled to have you aboard."

"Thank you!" Maribel's grip on my arm tightens. "Dot, this is my friend Eden, who I told you about. She's a whiz with a sewing machine."

"Eden." Dot turns her rainbow gaze on me. "The gymnast, right?"

I nod. "I'm really a total beginner. At sewing."

"We will take all the help we can get. Sotomayor Drama did

Joseph about five years ago, so we have most of the costumes already. But they'll need alternations to fit this cast. For example, our previous Pharaoh was about a foot taller than Maribel here!"

Maribel shrieks. "Wait—don't tell me—was it Fernando Montoya?!"

Dot reaches back and taps a photo behind her of a tall Latino boy in a white Elvis suit, his hair poufed up like the famous singer's, striking a pose exactly like Elvis in old movies I've seen.

"The one and only. Do you know Fernando?"

I think Maribel literally goes weak in the knees. Now she's gripping me just to stay standing. "He's in my sister's year at school. I've seen him in all the shows at the high school. He's amazing."

"Wait," I say, noticing that the plaque under the Elvis picture says *Joseph and the Amazing Technicolor Dreamcoat.* "That's . . . Pharaoh?" I was envisioning an Ancient Egyptian thing.

Maribel and Dot both laugh. "It'll make sense when you see the show," Dot says. "Eden, why don't you write your email address down for me and I'll be in touch about the costumes. Do you have your own sewing machine?"

When I get home, the Indian food has been cleared away and the only thing on the table is the fancy sewing machine. I drop my bags and sit down, inviting Blizz up into my lap while I examine the box.

I don't understand most of the features, but maybe it'll be good to have this. I'm not sure if Mom's old machine could have handled the heavy sequined fabric I saw in that Elvis photo.

After taking Blizz for a quick walk and getting a snack, I haul the machine up to the guest bedroom/new sewing room. I set it on the desk next to Mom's old machine. I wouldn't even know they were meant for the same basic activity. The new one has a touch screen and so many buttons, I think I might need Skye the NASA engineer to help me figure it out.

But there's a manual the size of my prealgebra textbook, so I settle on the bed and open it up.

By the time my stomach starts growling, I've managed to sew an impressive stack of pads. I'm not using any of the bells and whistles on the fancy machine and honestly could have made as many with the other one, but I'm hoping Mom will be happy.

Or at least not as mad at me as she was last night.

I bring the stack downstairs and start making a salad. I know there's some leftover roast chicken in there, so all I have to do is chop up some veggies and she'll be stunned at my cooking skills.

Sure enough, when she walks in around seven, the look on her face when she sees the table set and dinner ready is memorable. It's not just-won-regionals proud, but something close.

"Wow," she says. "This all looks great."

I brace for her to say she already ate with a client, or something about how she's off carbs and doesn't want the croutons on the salad.

But she makes some sort of decision in her head, then says, "Give me a minute to change?"

When she comes down, she's a whole new person. Hair down, face scrubbed clean, comfy clothes. And not the ultra-expensive comfy clothes that make her look like she's modeling for a You Can Have It All spread in a women's magazine. No, this time she has on a UW sweatshirt and flannel pants.

"Are you okay?" I ask as she pours a glass of wine.

"Of course. Why?"

Because you're dressed like a normal person who's in for the evening? Of course I don't say that.

"No, nothing."

She sits and digs into her salad. She eyes the stack of pads on the corner of the table but doesn't say anything, and I'm not ready to bring it up yet. Instead, I tell her about the musical and how Maribel and Julie are so excited to be cast.

"Who's Julie?" she asks.

So I tell her about this new group of friends I seem to have fallen into. She tells me about a mentorship program she's starting where she and some of her high-level executives partner with women just starting out with their own businesses.

When we're done eating, I get up to clear the dishes, but she waves me away.

"You cooked," she says. "I'll clean up."

I sit there for a minute, eyeing the pads. Finally, I hold up the stack and say, "I used the new machine to make these. It's really nice."

She nods, scooping the leftover salad into a storage container.

"I'm sorry I acted ungrateful," I say.

She nods again. "I get it. I do know what it's like to be poor, you know."

Of course I know that. Grandma still lives like they did when Mom was growing up. The difference is, Grandma is happy with her simple life. And I suppose Grandma can rely on Mom if she ever really needs help.

That's kind of a big difference I never really thought of before.

"It's just, I'm learning a lot at Casa Esperanza."

"I know," she says. "I'm glad you're having that experience. But I want you to know not everything is black and white. Sometimes the solutions that seem so simple, especially when you're young, are more complicated."

"I know that," I say. Except some things *are* black and white. People shouldn't be as rich as we are when so many people live on the streets.

"Like menstrual products for homeless people," she says. "You want me to solve that problem by donating MySecret products, but how? Homeless people don't have closets to hold boxes of free supplies. And your cloth pads are nice for environmental do-gooders, but homeless people don't have washing machines to keep them sanitary."

"I know, you already said that."

"I'm only saying there aren't easy answers. We're all doing our best."

But is she? Are we?

"It's not an easy answer, but I actually have an idea that could solve that problem. Well, not solve it. But it would be a start."

A flicker of annoyance passes over her face, but it's gone as soon as it came. "And what's that?"

"Well, it's not only my idea. It started with me, but then Will and Soledad helped—"

"Who's Soledad?"

"Maribel's sister. She's eighteen, so she's a registered voter. Which means she can propose an initiative for the ballot—"

Mom freezes, but she doesn't say anything, so I explain more about the tax on big companies that would pay for menstrual products in schools and community centers and other public places where homeless people could access them.

She's quiet for a minute after I'm done talking, and the only sound is the water running and the dishes jangling as she shoves them into the dishwasher. Finally, she says, "Menstrual products are already free in schools. That bill passed a while ago."

"I know!" I jump up, excited that she knows this. Finally, she'll understand what I'm trying to do. "The bill passed requiring schools to provide them. But it didn't fund them! How are schools supposed to pay for them? That's what my initiative would do!"

"Your initiative?" She gives up on the dishes, slamming the door to the dishwasher shut. "You're thirteen years old! You don't understand anything about corporate taxes and running a business and passing a law. These people are putting ideas into your head—"

"'These people'?"

"Maribel's family, and that boy, and what's her name, Sparrow?"

"It's Raven, and you know it!"

"I think you've spent about enough time with them."

"Are you serious?"

"All I am is serious. How else would I survive running a big, evil corporation that hates poor people?"

"I never said any of those things!"

"Believe it or not, being your mom is my most important job. No more Casa Esperanza. No more sewing circles. Starting now, you come home from school and do your homework and take care of this ridiculous dog, who, in case you've forgotten, is your responsibility!"

Blizz has been getting under her feet as he does anytime someone's in the kitchen and there's the chance they might drop something. She shoos him away, and I grab him, holding him close, like maybe he might calm my pounding heart.

"I cannot believe you're forbidding me to work at a food pantry!"

"It's all part of my plot for world domination," she snaps. "You don't understand now, but you'll get it when you're older. I'm keeping you safe from people I don't know who are filling your head with values I don't share and turning you against me. Good night, Eden."

Chapter Twelve

I can't pay attention in school the next day. Instead, I'm constantly replaying the fight with Mom the night before. How did we go from a pleasant meal together to her banning me from hanging out with the nicest friends I've ever had? And what parent ever has banned their kid from volunteering at a food bank?!

I spend lunchtime in the library, not because I'm avoiding Maribel to obey my mom. But because I'm afraid Maribel will ask me to go to Casa Esperanza after school or someone will ask me what's wrong, and how am I supposed to say my mom doesn't want me hanging out with you anymore? How would I explain that?

The irony is, Maribel isn't even involved in the activism stuff. She'd be a lot happier if I wasn't sewing pads or working with Will and Soledad on the initiative.

What am I going to tell Will and Soledad? The whole thing was basically my idea! And now Soledad is making it her senior project, which she needs to graduate. But I promised to help with it.

As a gymnast, I had commitments drilled into me from the time I was little. You show up for practice no matter what. It doesn't matter if you're sick or sleepy or if your grandpa just died. (I went straight from a funeral to a meet once, skipping the wake after.) You show up for yourself and for your team. For your coaches, who've put so much into you, and for your parents, who've spent so much money and time on your training.

Flaking out of responsibilities is not me. It's not my mom, either, honestly, but she's too busy being defensive to see that.

I'm waiting for my ride after school when I get a text. It's probably my mother, checking up on me to make sure I'm coming straight home.

But it's not my mom. It's Will.

Coming to CE today?

Can't.

:-(Soledad's here for a brainstorming session.

What do I tell him? I can't exactly say my mom thinks he and his mom are a bad influence.

I'm grounded.

??!?!

He could never possibly understand. Raven probably doesn't even believe in grounding. I bet she wants Will to learn from his mistakes and try and fail, and she would definitely never forbid him from volunteering at a food bank.

I'm heading home. I'll text you when I get there.

But once I'm home and I've dealt with Blizz, I don't text Will. I should. But I'm so frustrated to be letting them down. I'm in the guest room, cutting out more fabric for pads when my phone screen lights up with a video call.

"Eden!" Will's eyes are bright, while Soledad laughs in the background. "Why are you not here with us?"

Soledad laughs louder and the phone jostles for a moment. Will gets control back and shakes his head in mock seriousness. "We need your seriousness to focus us."

Is that how he sees me? Serious? Serious basically equals boring.

"I'm sorry." I put down the fabric scissors. "I'm supposed to come straight home after school."

"Isn't your mom always at work anyway?" Soledad leans into the picture. "Is she really going to know? I'd get you home in time."

"Not cool, Sol," Will says, recentering the phone on himself. "Eden is a lawful-good, parent-abiding person and we need to respect that. Besides, through the wonders of technology, she can still be here with us in our meeting!"

I try to ignore the part where Will basically called me boring again. Not that it matters. Whatever. Instead, I try to focus on the part where he wants me in the meeting.

"So what are you guys doing?"

"Drafting the initiative language," Soledad says, grabbing the phone and setting it up on the table in the CE classroom so I can see them both and the papers spread around them. "I've tracked down all the paperwork, and once we draft the language for the initiative, my adviser at school will look at it. Then we'll send it in and wait for its approval. Then we have until July 1 to get all the signatures we need."

My heart sinks. I don't know how I'm going to be able to help collect signatures outside grocery stores if I'm not allowed to leave the house except for school. How does my mom not realize how completely educational this is?! I'm learning about the democratic process!

"So basically two months," Will says. "Good thing you're not doing the play, like Maribel. She's going to have rehearsals all the time."

Soledad rolls her eyes. "She doesn't want to help anyway."

We get down to business, and together we figure out what we want the initiative to say. When we're done with the language, I expect them to hang up, but they don't. Soledad's working on home-work, but she chimes in every now and then as Will chats with me about teaching his bearded dragon to ride the robot vacuum.

After a while I set the phone up on the nightstand so I can finish cutting fabric. Also, maybe I want Will to see that I'm doing what I can to help too. He doesn't say anything, so when there's a lull in the conversation, I awkwardly say, "I'm making pads."

He grins. "That's cool. But we leave for Guatemala on Monday, so take your time getting any more sewing done for my mom."

A pang of disappointment strikes. Guatemala is really far away. "How long are you going to be gone?"

"One week," he says. "I'd text, but we won't have service."

"Who's going to watch Fyrian?" I ask, thinking of his scaly friend.

"Why? Are you volunteering?"

I shudder and he laughs. "Don't worry, there's a kid in the building who's super excited to feed him roaches."

We exchange email addresses, because he might have access to the internet occasionally. And he makes me promise to help Soledad with whatever she needs.

"Thanks, Will," I say as our conversation winds down.

"For what?"

I'm not even sure. I only know I feel so much more purpose working on this, and on Periods with Dignity, than I have in a long time.

"For not shutting down my idea, I guess."

"That was easy. It's a great idea."

Chapter Thirteen

Over the next week, Maribel's constantly busy with rehearsals for the musical. Lunchtime usually becomes an extended musical rehearsal while Skye and I sit as a sort of captive audience while she and Julie sing and go over choreography the whole time. But at least I have some idea what they're talking about, since Dot has started giving me small tasks for the show's costumes, like hemming things and replacing buttons. Skye's busy too, with her lacrosse season heating up. And of course, Will's in Guatemala.

It's not like I'd be allowed to hang out with any of them anyway, so instead, I sew pads for hours every afternoon. Sometimes Soledad calls with updates on the initiative. Her adviser at school approved our draft of the language, and she got it submitted to the Office of the Secretary of State.

"Have you heard from Will?" she asks, one day after an unsuccessful brainstorming session, trying to figure out a hashtag for our campaign. It seems a little soon to be worrying about that when we don't even know if we'll be approved to petition, and even then we don't know if it'll make it on the ballot. But unbridled enthusiasm seems to run in the Miller-Paz family. For Maribel, it's theater. For Silvia, it's Casa Esperanza. For Flor, it's whatever the bigger girls are doing.

And for Soledad, it seems like it's this project. My idea. Something that could help a lot of people.

"No, I haven't heard from him yet."

"Well, don't worry. Mom's only heard from Raven once, but it sounds like things are going well. And he'll be back soon!"

I'm not sure why she thinks I'd worry, but I don't mind the big sisterliness. Soledad and Carmen may drive Maribel crazy, but she doesn't realize how good she has it.

Says the girl currently sitting in an empty house (again), except for the bonkers little dog who has finally settled, this time in the middle of the fabric I need to start cutting.

Dot has me making actual costumes for the show now. They're incredibly simple—basic beige tunics that everyone will wear over leggings as their base costume, and then put different robes and accessories on over them. So basically they're two big rectangles sewn together, with a neckhole and two armholes. Completely shapeless, but I'm pretty proud the first time I finish one and try it on.

I made something from start to finish. Someone will wear it onstage. No one's going to be like, "Who crafted that incredible tunic?" But still, I'll know.

By the time Will's week in Guatemala is almost up, I've received one email from him:

Hey, Eden! I only have a minute in this
internet café. Things are going well
here. We've distributed lots of pads and
done some workshops teaching how to make
them. My Spanish is improving. Un poqui-
to! See you soon!

On Friday I deliver a stack of tunics to Dot, who doesn't have
another project ready for me to take home yet. So I head to lunch
feeling kind of bereft, a whole weekend ahead of me with nothing
to do.

"Hi!" Maribel greets me with more warmth than she's shown
in a while as she sits at the lunch table, not obsessing over *Joseph*
with Julie for once. "How's it going?"

"Good," I say. But I'm irritated. I never know what I'm going
to get with Maribel. After Graham, we were insta-best-friends. I
thought maybe I was going to have a social life after gymnastics.
But then things took a turn, because I didn't turn out to be exactly
who she wanted me to be.

"My mom misses you around Casa Esperanza," she says,
opening a yogurt. "But Sol says you've been a big help with her
project."

It's not her project, I almost say, but don't. Anyway, it is. Her
name will be on the initiative.

"I think it's pretty weird that you want to hang out with her,"
she says, "but better you than me." Before I've figured out what
to say to that, Maribel goes on. "And Dot can't stop raving about
how great you are with the costumes! I'm so glad you got involved
with the show."

"Me too," I say. And even if I can't quite figure Maribel out, I mean that.

Skye arrives with minutes to spare in the lunch period.

"Where've you been?" Julie asks as Skye unwraps her sandwich.

"Overslept, missed my first-period bio quiz, had to make it up during lunch," she says, and then takes an enormous bite.

Since she's clearly going to devote these last couple of minutes to eating, not talking, the other two return to *Joseph* talk.

But Skye takes a moment between bites to ask, "How are you?"

"Me? Oh, I'm okay."

She sneaks a furtive glance at Maribel and Julie, who aren't paying us any attention. "Bit lonely lately?" she asks.

My eyebrows shoot up. She comes right out and says the things I'm always thinking but wouldn't say.

"I mean, I'm sure you have other stuff going on," she says. "But I know when Julie's in a show, I kind of lose her for a couple of months."

"Yeah."

She jams the last bit of sandwich in her mouth and chews comically. When it's gone, she says, "Hey, I don't know if this would interest you at all, but I have a lacrosse tournament this weekend. Would you maybe wanna . . ."

When I don't answer right away, she says, "Never mind, sorry, that was a dumb idea. I just thought since you're an athlete, but lacrosse—"

"No, I'd love to," I say. "I'm not sure if I can, though. I'm kinda . . . grounded? But not? I don't know. I have to check with my mom."

"Okay." The bell rings, and Skye takes a long drink from her water bottle, washing down her rapid-fire lunch. "Cool. I'll send you the details."

Which is how I end up on the sidelines of a lacrosse field on a wet Saturday morning in early May.

Mom had no problem with me going and even dropped me off on her way to a Pilates class. As long as something doesn't include Maribel's or Will's families, I guess it's okay. Unlikely that I'll get any wacky political ideas here. (Although you never know, making sports spectators stand on a muddy field without shelter or even bleachers should be illegal.)

Uncomfortable though it is, there's something familiar I hadn't realized I'd missed. Rooting for a team, together with strangers who are also rooting for your team, or maybe even against it, but all of you are invested in what's happening out there on the field, how hard the athletes are working, how all their training is paying off.

I've watched gymnastics on TV since I had to quit, but it's been a long time since I've sat in the stands (gymnastics: a reasonable sport that happens indoors, with seats) and watched other athletes put everything on the line. There's a different energy when you're right there; you can hear the grunt of effort, see the sweat trickling down a forehead.

You're close enough to see that that athlete has a Star of David necklace, and that one has purple nail polish. They're real people bringing their own stuff to this field, working through their own injuries or mental hang-ups. They'll go home and ice their knees or backs or shoulders and celebrate or comfort themselves with their carb of choice.

Mine was always ice cream bars, the ones with vanilla inside and dark chocolate outside.

With that thought, I'm there, remembering not only what it was like to be a spectator, but also to be one of those athletes, giving everything to the sport I loved (even when I sometimes hated it). And not only what it felt like to be an individual athlete, either, but what it felt like to be part of a team.

There's Skye, her braids pulled back in a bright blue wrap that matches her team's jerseys. She's just assisted on a goal (or whatever it's called in lacrosse), and she and her teammate who made the goal do a double high five, both beaming.

I whoop for her from the sidelines, and she waves at me as she runs back into the fray.

Gymnasts are alone on the floor or the vault or the beam. That's part of what I loved about it—your success or failure is yours and yours alone. But you also know that no matter what happens in those moments when it's all you, your teammates are going to be there as soon as you step off the mat. They're going to be at your side while you wait for the scores to come in.

And the coaches are going to be there with a hug, a pat on the back, no matter what. They're going to look you in the eyes and tell you how great you did, how much you improved. Even if it was a total disaster, they'll find something good to mention, and then later, when you're ready for it, you'll talk about what you could do better next time.

"That's right, ladies!" Skye's coach hollers. "Good hustle!"

"Go Monarchs!" I yell, feeling free, feeling something break open inside me that had been stuck for too long.

At their break midway through, Skye comes running over to me.

"You came!"

"I did!"

"Are you miserable? Sorry it's so rainy."

"Yeah, you really should have arranged better weather."

Her face flickers before she realizes I'm joking, then she grins and leans down to retie her shoe. "Did you see Russell? Russell Meyer?"

It takes me a minute to process her name, even though I've competed with Russell for almost a decade. "She's here?"

"Her older sister is the coach." Skye points out tiny Russell, bundled up like it's the dead of winter, at the other end of the field. "I thought you might know her."

"Yeah." Probably she can feel us watching her because right then, Russell turns our way and her mouth makes a little O of recognition.

"Well, thanks for coming," Skye says.

"Of course. Thanks for inviting me."

Skye waves and runs back toward her teammates. I send her off with another whoop of support.

I wonder for a second if I could possibly get away without talking to Russell, but she's heading my way. So I meet her halfway.

"Eden, hi!" she says in this big, exaggerated way, like we were BFFs. "I thought that might be you, but the way you were cheering, I wasn't sure?"

I'm not sure what that means. Like I didn't support my gymnastics teammates? That's not true. But I guess it is true that I never would have whooped and shouted my encouragement. I was more of a nods and smiles and quiet "nice jobs" kind of teammate. It didn't mean I was any less sincere, though.

I shrug. "Just supporting my friend. Your sister is the coach?"

Russell nods. "When she got too tall for gymnastics, she switched to lacrosse. I don't make it to very many games, but I was free today."

If I had a sister who coached a team, I could make it to every single game now. "Congrats on Classics," I say, trying to bite back the feeling that we both know I would have won her gold on bars if I'd been there. "That was an amazing Jaeger." Her release move really was amazing. But not as amazing as mine used to be.

"Thanks," she says, her gaze drifting off toward the field, where they've started the second half. "We miss you around the gym," she finally says.

"I miss being there."

We exchange an awkward hug, and she heads back over toward her mom, who waits with a travel mug of something hot.

I'm left to wonder if that was true, what I said. Do I miss being in the gym? If I really did, I could go back. I could volunteer with the Tots, or transition to rhythmic gymnastics, which is more dance than acrobatics.

The thing is, I'm not sure I really do miss it. I don't miss the long workouts. I don't miss the ice packs and heat packs and constant massage and chiropractor appointments. At some point, even before my injury, it stopped being fun and started weighing on me so much that even when I was flying through the air, I felt chained down.

But standing here on this grim, rainy day, watching Skye and her teammates work together and celebrate one another's accomplishments and help each other up when they fall down, I realize that's what I've been missing. Feeling like I'm a part of something. Working with a team, with the same goal, the same urgency to achieve it.

My phone buzzes with a text. It's Sol, asking if I can make a meeting on Monday. In person. We really need you there, she says. And it's not the same as a gymnastics team, or a lacrosse team, but maybe I do have something urgent to accomplish.

Monday after school, Soledad is waiting for me in the beat-up clunker she and Carmen share with Silvia. Will grins at me from the backseat.

"Hi!" he says as I climb in the front. "How was your day of conventional schooling?"

"Pretty boring," I say, twisting around in my seat to see him. "Welcome back! How was it?"

"Amazing!" He chatters nonstop about the trip as Soledad drives us to Will's apartment for our brainstorming session. When Mom first told me I had to come straight home after school, I thought she might check my phone location. But if she did, she never mentioned it. And I'm gambling that if she did in the beginning, she's stopped, since I've proven trustworthy.

(At least until now.)

"We went to this one village," Will explains, "where we had to take this rickety little water taxi across this lake, and the waters were super choppy. I stood up to take a picture and almost fell out. When we got to the village, we went to this organization where they teach traditional Guatemalan weaving techniques to tourists, and then my mom gave them a bunch of materials and our patterns and showed them how to make pads. She had some of yours as samples."

"Whoa. Really?" That's amazing to think that something I made could impact someone in a whole other country.

"And we went to other villages, and some schools and community centers in the capital, which is huge. Everyone was so nice, and the food was amazing."

"¿Y cómo está tu español ahora?" Soledad asks. "¿Ya hablas como un chapín de verdad?"

Will blinks slowly at her. Then he says in what even I can tell is a terrible accent, "Quiero más comida, por favor."

She laughs and drops us in front of the apartment building, then goes off to search for a parking spot.

"Why are we here instead of Casa Esperanza?" I ask as Will unlocks the door to the lobby.

"Oh, Sol's invited a few other people, so we figured we'd have more space here." He sees something in my face. "Is that okay? I know this is sort of your project—"

"It's really not—"

"No, but it was your idea—"

"Yeah, but now it's Soledad's senior project. So."

Will's quiet for a minute as he lets us into their apartment, which smells like cinnamon and incense. He shows me where to drop my backpack and leads me to the kitchen.

"But seriously. Are you okay with it? I hope we didn't get carried away while you were grounded."

"No," I say, and I mean it. "I think it's great. It's a huge project.

We need all the help we can get!"

Will pulls out some snacks—fruit and seaweed chips and a dish of vegan brownies. He's getting me a natural soda and opening a kombucha for himself when Sol buzzes to be let in. By the time she arrives, she's got three more people in tow, all of whom look like older high schoolers.

"Look who I found hanging around outside," she says. "This is Cole, Verity, and Fernando."

Cole has dark hair that's super short on the sides and long and floppy on top, and a prominent pin that says THEY/THEM.

Verity is white, with waist-length blond hair and a Shorewood Cheer varsity jacket. She gives a little wave.

And Fernando is a tall, handsome Latino guy who launches into a complicated handshake with Will. "Good to see you again, man," he says. Then turns to me, saying, "And nice to meet you . . . ?"

"Eden," Will supplies.

"Right, sorry." Soledad bustles in and starts spreading her stuff out on the dining room table. "This whole thing was Eden's idea, and she's graciously letting me butt in for my senior project."

"No, I couldn't have done it by myself. I mean, not just because I'm not old enough to vote."

Once everyone is settled around the table with the snacks in the middle, Soledad takes charge. "The excellent news is that we heard back about the petition language. It's been approved!"

"Nice!" Will holds up his hands for a high five, and I'm reminded of Skye and her lacrosse teammates.

"The . . . challenging news is that we're going to need 325,000 unique signatures by July 1 to get it on the November ballot."

"So a little less than two months," Cole says, fiddling with a chunky beaded bracelet.

"Exactly, and considering everyone's different schedules with sports and cheer and shows, we're probably going to need to do it mostly on the weekends. So I think we should get started this coming weekend. Does that work for everyone?"

The high schoolers pull out their phones to consult their calendars. Will shrugs. "I'm in," he says.

"I have a show Saturday night and a Sunday matinee," Fernando says. "But I'm open on Sunday night and could do anytime before six on Saturday."

"I'm free," Cole says.

"I have a work shift on Saturday, but I can get it covered," Verity says.

Everyone turns to me.

"Oh, um." A whole day on a weekend is going to be a lot trickier than a few hours after school when my mom's guaranteed to be at work. And how much do they really need me? Will and Soledad are so charming that between the two of them, they could probably fill up the entire petition.

Then again, 325,000 is a lot of signatures.

And my palm still tingles from where Will high-fived me.

"Yeah, I'll figure it out."

"Okay, so I'll send out a group text and we'll create a schedule. Moving on!"

Soledad turns it over to Verity, who has apparently worked on initiative campaigns before, to explain best practices for gathering signatures. We're allowed by law in public places. But on private property, like outside a grocery store, the owner has rights to restrict political activity.

"But they don't, usually," Verity says at the horrified look on my face. I'm envisioning some angry store owner yelling at me to get off his property. "The main thing is to be polite and friendly, and never be pushy. If people say no, even if they're rude, you back off. That way, no one complains to the owner, and the owners will be chill. That's the way it's always worked for me."

Fernando reaches across me for the platter of brownies. "Sorry," he says with a little smile. "What if they give fake names?" he asks. "You know, Ivana Tinkle, Seymour Butts . . . ?"

"You mean like you did when I petitioned for compostable straws in the cafeteria?" Soledad leans across the table, getting in Fernando's face.

"Exactly." He grins and gives a mock bow of apology. "We were in seventh grade, to be fair. That was the height of hilarity then."

"I mean, these two are in seventh grade," Soledad says, motioning toward Will and me.

Fernando turns his apology bow to us. "Clearly, they are much more mature and intelligent than I've ever been."

"But it's a good question," Verity says, getting us back on topic. "Because it happens a lot. Mostly people aren't malicious. They'd just rather write down a fake name than say no. Also, some names will be invalid because it'll turn out they're not registered voters."

"So those won't count toward the 325,000 signatures?" Soledad says.

"Right. The suggestion is to get around twenty percent more signatures than you think you need."

Cole whips out their phone. "So that means . . . 390,000."

We all sit with that number for a moment. Fernando takes another brownie. "Looks like we've got some work to do," he says.

The next day at lunch Maribel slams her hands down on the table as soon as I arrive.

"You hung out with Fernando Montoya?!" she screeches.

People all around us turn to stare. I freeze, unsure if Maribel is angry or excited or what. Also trying to figure out what she is talking about.

"Um . . ."

"Don't deny it. Will already told me. I can't believe you didn't tell me! Fernando Montoya! Guh. Did he sing?!"

"Fernando from our initiative meeting?" I ask, sitting down. "No, he didn't sing."

"But he sat next to you. Will said."

Next to her, Julie squeaks.

I mean, there's no denying Fernando is super cute, in a way-too-old-for-me way. But these two are in deep.

"He's nice, but we weren't exactly hanging out. It was a meeting about Soledad's senior project."

"Yeah, yeah, ballot initiatives blah blah blah," Maribel says. "I might even put up with all that to hang out with Fernando Montoya!"

"Well . . . you're welcome to join us."

"Right." Maribel throws an annoyed eye roll at Julie, who looks warily between us, like she doesn't want to be involved.

"What does that mean? You are. We invited you."

"Who's we? You and my sister? Or you and my oldest friend? Because apparently you spend all your time with the two of them."

Eyes wide, Julie stands and pulls Skye with her, mumbling something about going to see if there's any chocolate milk left.

Maribel's looking at me, expectantly, waiting for me to say something.

"I don't know why you're mad," I finally say. "We did invite you. And you've been busy with the play."

"It's a good thing," she says. "Because I've pretty much lost you to the activism side."

"You haven't lost me. . . ." I trail off, because I don't know what else to say. She was the one who dropped me for the show. And while it stung a little, I got that. Maybe because in gymnastics friendships, everyone always understands that gymnastics comes first, friendships second. So no one's feelings are hurt if they're in second place, because everyone is.

"Well, it'd be nice to see you sometime when you aren't plotting with Will and Soledad about how to change the world."

I'd like that too. But the reality is, I'm not even allowed to see Maribel outside of school. So it's not like I can figure out a time for us to hang.

When Julie and Skye come back, the awkward silence turns to talk of the show at a local theater that Fernando's currently starring in. That's when it clicks for me. The photo of the tall middle schooler playing Pharaoh on Dot's wall of show photos.

"Oh, he played your part, right?"

Julie turns to me, gobsmacked. "Um, yes! I can't believe you've never seen him perform. You have to come with us to see his show on Friday night. You too," she says to Skye. "Let's all go! It's *Big Fish*, and he's playing Edward Bloom!"

Skye and I exchange blank looks.

"*Big Fish* is so good," Maribel says, unable to resist musical theater talk. "The music is amazing, and Edward Bloom is this larger-than-life character who's always telling tall tales and making romantic gestures."

"Daffodils!" Julie squeals, and then she and Maribel belt out a line from some song about daffodils.

"You could all sleep over at my house after," Maribel says, looking a little bit hopeful.

"I could do the show," Skye says. "But I have to be up super early for lacrosse on Saturday morning."

I obviously can't sleep over at Maribel's house. Plus, I have Saturday plans too. I haven't figured out how on Earth I'm going to make them happen, though.

"What about you, Eden?"

Maribel's looking at me like this is a test.

"I want to," I say slowly. "But my mom's been super strict about where I go and what I do lately." Maribel frowns. I know that sounds vague, like I'm trying to back out without saying why. "I'm basically grounded," I say, since that's the easiest explanation.

"What'd you do?" Julie asks, reaching into Maribel's bag of pretzels and snagging one for herself.

"It doesn't matter," Maribel says. "It's just an excuse."

With that, she tosses her pretzels to Julie and storms away from the table.

My throat tightens and my eyes well up, but I breathe through it. If I could compete through a torn labrum, I can suck this up. I'm just so thrown. Will said things with Maribel were black and white. I guess that means if I can't be her very best friend in the world at all times, I can't be her friend at all.

Mom wants me to clear the sewing stuff out of the guest room so Olga can change the sheets for Grandma. I usually keep my mess contained to my bedroom, but I have to admit I've let the guest room get a bit out of control. Mom leaves on Thursday and will be gone all weekend for some Women in Leadership conference in Vancouver, which means Grandma is coming to stay.

"Why can't she stay in the third-floor guest room?"

"Because her knees are acting up and one flight of stairs is going to be tricky enough for her. Plus, this way she'll be closer to you."

Grandma is supposedly going to be here to take care of me, but if she struggles to get up stairs, I'm pretty sure I'm going to do more taking care of her. Still, it will be nice to have someone around. Who actually likes to, I don't know, talk to me.

So I haul the bins full of *Joseph* costumes Dot gave me to hem and mend, plus the bins of supplies for pads, up one more flight of stairs to the third-floor guest room.

I almost never come up here. No one does, except maybe Olga. But it's a kind of great room. It's the entire attic, wide open, with sloped ceilings and skylights and tons of space to spread out.

I make a couple of more trips for the sewing machine and other supplies, then grab my phone and computer from my bedroom and set up camp in the attic.

"Where are you?" Will asks when he video calls that evening.

"My new sewing room." I hold up a pad I just finished sewing.

"Like, in your house?"

"Yeah, it's the attic."

"It looks awesome. Why isn't that your room?"

I look around at the room that's big enough to hold all my stuff plus an entire sewing workshop. It's a little stiff and formal now because it's decorated like a magazine guest room. But I could make it my own pretty easily.

"You know, maybe it will be," I say. "Is there any initiative news?"

He shakes his head. "You know everything I know! Saturday morning, right?"

"Right." Soledad's schedule puts me and Will together with official adult/registered voter Fernando at the Trader Joe's right off Aurora. She and Verity will be at the Central Market, and Cole and their boyfriend will be at the PCC.

"What's wrong?" Will asks. "Are you nervous?"

"No." I'm totally nervous. Finally, I can't hold it in any longer. "Look, can I tell you something?"

Will sets down the fidget spinner he was fiddling with and leans in. "Of course. Anything."

"I'm not supposed to be doing this. I'm not allowed."

"That's why we have eighteen-year-olds helping."

"No. I mean, my mom doesn't want me working on this at all."

"Oh." He pauses. "Is she worried about someone confronting us or something?"

"No." Just like with Maribel, I can't tell him my mom doesn't approve of him and his family. But I can tell him at least part of it. "It's the politics of it."

"She's against . . . the democratic process?"

"No!" I laugh. "I mean, it seems like that, doesn't it? But she's the CEO of a large company."

"A corporation."

"Yeah. A menstrual products corporation."

"So . . . she doesn't want menstrual products to be free?"

"It's not even that. It's bigger issues about believing the government shouldn't put controls on businesses, that private businesses and individuals should be the ones to fund social needs like this one. And MySecret does donate products. But that it shouldn't be the government Robin Hooding money from the corporations to pay for stuff for the people."

I only know this because I went online and found some videos of her giving talks at conferences like the one she's going to this weekend.

"What's your excuse to get out, then?"

"Doing stuff for the musical. At least this weekend she'll be out of town. My grandma's staying with me."

"Is she cool?"

"She is, but I don't want to make her lie for me. I can probably get away with telling her there's a rehearsal on a weekend. My mom's going to be in Canada, so she's not going to be tracking my phone."

"She does that?" Will looks astounded.

"I know, your mom would never."

"Well." His mouth quirks up in a strange smile. "She's not perfect either, you know."

I can't imagine what Raven's flaws are. But I know everyone's got stuff with their parents. "I know."

Finally, it's Friday night. Grandma and I have been having a great time since she arrived on Thursday afternoon. She pretty much lives in the one comfy chair in the living room, and Blizz pretty much lives on her lap. "What're we going to do for dinner tonight, sugar?" she says. "I should've brought some tray suppers."

"No, that's okay, Grandma." Last night we had some leftover catering that Mom had brought home from MySecret before she left for her conference. "Let me see what we've got."

"We can order pizza!" she calls as I go into the kitchen to survey what's in the fridge.

But I don't want to order food. I know my mom left a credit card for exactly that reason, but I also know Grandma won't use it. She'll peel cash off the wad folded up in an envelope that she always uses as a bookmark in whatever she's reading. And she only has so much of that cash.

But the pickings are slim in the kitchen. I pull together a plate of crackers, cheese, baby carrots, and orange slices. It would never fly as dinner with Mom, but Grandma doesn't bat an eye when I bring it out and set it between us in front of the TV.

Grandma has chosen a program about an old lady who writes mystery novels but also solves actual murders that happen in her tiny town. In this episode, there's a nosy tourist girl who keeps getting underfoot in the investigation. Grandma keeps chuckling when the girl appears, saying things like, "Well, she sure reminds me of someone we both know."

Except I'm not sure. She doesn't mean me—I've never been one to talk to strangers and make their business my own. And Grandma and I don't know too many people in common.

"Do you mean Mom?" I ask her as the end credits roll.

"Hmm?" she says, scanning the menu for what to watch next.

"Did you mean that little girl was like Mom?"

"I sure did!" She sets the remote down. "Always knew exactly what she wanted, your mom. Never settled for anything less. Never let anyone tell her something wasn't possible."

I guess that does sound like my mom. But I've never thought about what that looked like when she was a kid. "Did she get into a lot of trouble?"

Grandma chuckles again, like she did when she was watching the show. "Her fair share, yep. And I don't blame her. The trailer was small. She had to get out and find other things to do. If it was something I suggested, shoot! Forget it. No, it always had to be her way or the highway."

It's funny to think about my mom like that. Sneaking out and breaking rules, trouble making around the trailer park.

"Never solved any murders that I know of, though," Grandma says with a cackle as she presses play on the next episode.

I can't pay attention to the episode about the author's old flame who may or may not be the prime suspect. My wheels are turning too quickly. All week I've been wondering if I should back out of petitioning on Saturday. Even if my mom didn't strictly forbid that specific activity, it definitely falls under the category of ideas and values Mom doesn't share.

But from what Grandma said, standing up for what I believe in and going out and working for what I want is exactly what Mom herself would do.

I text Will:

Can you pick me up tomorrow morning?

Chapter Fourteen

As soon as I climb into Raven's car, Will blurts, "I couldn't sleep!"

"Me either!"

Raven laughs from the front seat. "You're going to regret that after a few hours on your feet."

"Any tips?" I ask. Raven's done this a bunch before. The only reason she's not helping on this campaign is that Periods with Dignity is busy getting ready to start a new donation drive with some of the really big companies in the Seattle area.

Raven tells us the same things Verity did—be friendly, but not pushy; get more signatures than you think you'll need; and she adds the advice to stay hydrated and take snack breaks.

We get there right as Fernando is pulling into the lot. "That's your supervising adult?" Raven asks at the sight of him unfolding himself from a tiny car and dropping his stack of clipboards on the ground.

"He's eighteen?" I say.

She bites back a laugh and walks over to introduce herself and give Fernando her number in case of emergency. As Raven heads back to her car, Fernando turns to us with his dazzling smile. "All right, Team Trader Joe's! Let's get some signatures!"

He goes inside to introduce himself to the manager, which Verity recommended. Will and I each take a clipboard and position ourselves between the door and the parking lot.

I scan the official-looking language on the petition, and then all the blank lines for signatures. Pages and pages of blank lines. How are we going to fill them all?

Will elbows me and I look up. "Someone's coming," he whispers.

It's awkward, seeing the person from across the lot. We know they're there, and they know we're here, and it's weird to watch them and weird to ignore them.

Will turns to me. "Should we pretend to be talking about something super interesting?" he says.

I let out a nervous giggle. "Yeah, it should probably look really mature and governmenty, too."

He cracks up, and then we've killed enough time that the person is nearly upon us.

We both hesitate, but right before it's too late, Will says, "Hi, could I tell you about—"

The person puts up their hand and keeps walking, throwing a "No thanks," over their shoulder.

"You hate to see it," Fernando says as he comes out in time to witness our failure. "Let the master show you how it's done."

The next person to approach is about eighty years old.

"Well, hello there, young lady," Fernando says, stepping forward to gallantly help her maneuver her walker over the curb.

"Could I possibly trouble you for a signature on this petition we've got here? It's for a school project."

She listens, entranced, as Fernando explains in clear, simple terms, and she signs happily. As she makes her way inside the store, Fernando turns to us with his arms spread wide, as if to say, "Easy as pie!"

"Beginner's luck," Will says. And then it's on.

Fernando moves to the other door, while Will and I stay teamed up, with a plan to compare signatures in an hour. Will doesn't hesitate on the next person who comes to our door, and they sign without even listening to the cause. But the next person wants to know more and I stumble through an explanation.

It's about half and half, the people who'll sign and the people who won't. The ones who won't aren't against the cause, or at least they don't say so. It's more that they don't want to be bothered. After the fourth or fifth pass, it stops stinging so much.

Then we get fraternity dude. At least, I assume, based on his ball cap with Greek letters on it.

"Are you a registered voter?" Will asks.

The guy stops, doing an exaggerated double take. Then he barks out a laugh. "Yeah, little man. I am. Are you?" Then he laughs like he's made the most hilarious joke. Over at his door, Fernando looks up from his conversation with a middle-aged woman to keep an eye on our situation.

"Just a concerned citizen," Will says smoothly, then moves into his explanation of the petition.

"I'm sorry, what?" the guy says. "Free . . . period stuff? Why should I pay for period products? I'm a dude."

"As am I," Will says.

"Yeah, but you're not a taxpayer, junior."

Thankfully, he considers that a cool exit line and saunters into the store. Across the way, Fernando shoots us a questioning look with a thumbs-up or -down gesture. We both give him a thumbs-up, then turn to smile at the mother with a baby and a toddler heading our way.

"I just can't," she says before we can even say a word.

When our hour is up, we go into the store, where Fernando buys us drinks and a package of cookies, and we sit on the curb a ways off from the doors.

"So," Fernando says. "How'd you do?"

We pull out our petitions and take a look. "Thirty-three, between us," Will says.

"Not bad," Fernando says.

"How many did you get?" I ask.

He looks a little shifty, but also he's dying to tell us.

"Come on, we can take it."

"Forty-nine," he finally says.

Will shrugs. "Well, we can't all be Mr. Personality."

"Hey, don't sell yourselves short. You did great. I saw you handle some difficult customers. That frat boy?" He shakes his head.

"What should our answer be to that, though?" I say. "He said he shouldn't have to pay for period products because he's a dude."

"Well, first of all," Will says, "the tax is on companies, not individuals. So the initiative doesn't actually ask him to pay for anything."

"And we're not even asking him to vote for it. Only support adding it to the ballot," Fernando points out. "But if I were arguing the principal of taxpayer-funded period products, I'd say that our taxes pay for schools, whether or not we have kids. Libraries, whether or not we use them. Roads and bridges in parts of the state where we'll never drive. Something doesn't have to directly benefit you to be worth doing."

The afternoon hums along much like the morning did. I'd probably get bored or bummed by all the no's if I was on my own. But with Will at my side, we keep it fun. And somehow, even though he's on his own, Fernando keeps it fun too. When there's a lull, he tap dances. And he's so good at charming the customers, joking with them and drawing them in with his whole magnetic thing.

I forget to check in with Grandma until Raven calls Will around three. I shoot a quick text to Grandma, letting her know I'm doing fine. She sends me back a picture of Blizz sleeping on her lap. Who knew that the way to get Blizz to chill out was to sit still with him all day?

By the end of the day, we've gathered an impressive number of signatures. We video call Soledad and gather around Fernando's car with our clipboards stacked on his trunk.

"So?" he says, when Soledad answers. "How badly did we beat you?"

"You wish," she says, a shriek of laugher in the background. "Verity and I got a hundred and three signatures today. How about you?"

Fernando grins and holds up both hands for Will and me to high-five. "One eighty-five," Will announces, the pride obvious in his voice.

"Whoa, nice!" Sol says.

"Well, I don't mean to throw a bucket of ice water on the celebration," Cole interrupts, poking their head into the picture, "but with mine and Micah's, today we got three hundred fifty-four signatures. And if we take out the twenty percent that are likely invalid, that's only two hundred eighty-three. Out of almost four hundred thousand."

Everyone's quiet for a minute.

In the quiet, I get a text. Not from Grandma but my mom.

Conference going well, but I miss you! Hope you're having fun with Grandma.

I should respond, but then Soledad speaks, her voice commanding.

"Then we have to step it up. Not just weekends. And we've got to recruit more people."

After spending all day talking and laughing, we're quiet as Fernando drives us home. But it's a nice quiet. When we reach my house, Will steps out of the car and walks me to the door. Which is definitely a thing friends do.

"Do you think we're going to make it?" he asks.

"What?"

"To the number of signatures we need," he says. He scuffs his toe on the ground, suddenly awkward.

"Oh. I sure hope so."

"Yeah. Me too." He shoots me one last smile and lopes back to Fernando's car.

Chapter Fifteen

I feel terrible all day Sunday as the team text chain plans out the week's petitioning shifts. There's no way I can get away with it every day after school. Maybe once or twice I could say there was costume stuff to do, but Mom and I have had a tentative peace since she returned, and I don't want to risk it.

The bright side of spending most of my time at home is that when my period starts again a couple of days later, I'm sitting at the sewing machine in the attic, sewing pads.

Instead of panicking and asking every menstruator in the vicinity for help, I calmly go to the little basket of cloth pads I've made for myself—the wonky ones with mistakes, mostly. I mean, no one else is going to see them, so who cares?

I rinse the stained underwear like Sol told me to do with my jeans, then put them in my laundry bin and snap a pad into a fresh pair. Then I'm back to sewing. If everyone else is out there working hard to get signatures, I'm going to make more pads than any one person has ever made for Periods with Dignity.

I know I can't solve period poverty on my own. No one person can. Even my mom's entire company couldn't solve it, because it's not just about supplying products. It's about whole systems that are built only to support certain people.

Sol showed me this essay from this old feminist lady Gloria Steinem about how the world would be different if cis men had periods—how they'd brag about their periods, and celebrities would put their faces on products, and supplies would obviously be free.

She wrote this in the 1980s! And here we are, forty years later, and nothing has changed! I mean, the world has changed in a gazillion ways, but not on this issue. We've got cell phones and internet and hashtags—

Wait—hashtags.

Without giving myself a chance to think about whether or not this is totally stupid, I pull out my phone and open up the group text.

The next day, Soledad picks me up after school, Will grinning at me from the passenger seat again.

"You've outdone yourself this time, Eden," Sol says, pulling away from the curb and nearly colliding with a school bus as she does. "I really think this is going to make the difference!"

"I hope so." I don't want to oversell my idea, in case it doesn't work, but I can't stop the bloom of pleasure at Soledad's praise. "Where are we going?" I ask when we pass the turnoff for Will's apartment building.

"Verity's," Will says, twisting around in his seat. "She has more room, and we've recruited more people."

I was thinking maybe a couple of Raven's activist friends, but when we walk into Verity's, the room is packed. I recognize Vincent and LuAnn and Samira from the sew-along, but I think most of the new people are high schoolers.

"Yay! Eden!" Verity literally jumps up and down and claps her hands when she sees me. She runs over, hugs me, and pulls me to stand with her in front of the fireplace. "Hey! Pipe down!" she booms in her cheerleader voice.

Everyone goes quiet and turns our way.

"Okay, so, this is Eden. Coolest middle schooler you've ever met."

"Hey!" Will protests.

"Next to Will over there," she concedes.

"Hey!" I protest, barely able to believe when it comes out of my mouth, but the laugh I get in response is worth it.

"Equally as cool as Will," Verity amends. "This whole initiative was her idea, and now she's had another strike of inspiration on how to get more signatures. Want to explain, Eden?"

I would have preferred Verity explain, or Will. They both would do much better. But if I'm going to channel Mom in getting what I want, I have to channel her in this, too.

"Okay, so, hi." I take a breath. Soledad is probably trying to be encouraging when she lets out a whoop, but it just puts more pressure on me. "Um, so, I used to be a gymnast. And I was thinking about the most recent Olympic team, how there were social media campaigns to support them—"

"Did you go to the Olympics?" someone perched on the edge of the couch asks.

"No—"

"She almost did," Will says.

I shake off my irritation at that assumption, yet again. "Anyway, that's not the point. The point is, there were hashtags that supported the team, and that's where fans knew to look for the latest news, but also where the gymnasts could look for support—"

"I'm not sure how a hashtag's going to get you hundreds of thousands of signatures," says a tiny blond-haired girl who looks way too perky to sound so glum.

Soledad stands up next to me. "Would you let her finish?"

"You're right," I say, when everyone's quiet again. "A hashtag alone isn't enough. What we need the most is bodies. Volunteers to petition over the next six weeks, not only in Seattle but across the state."

"And the hashtag will recruit the volunteers?" Micah asks.

"Yes, but not just the hashtag. Even if everyone here used the hashtag a bunch every day, that wouldn't be enough to really make an impact."

"It might," says the glum girl. "I have twelve thousand Instagram followers."

"Okay, well that's a good start. But I was thinking that we have to go viral. I know you can't just decide to go viral, but I was thinking about what kinds of content are most likely to get people's attention—"

"I love that parrot who can swear in six languages," someone offers.

"Or that cat who predicts the weather," someone else says.

"Does anyone have a super-talented pet?" Cole asks.

Will stands and lets out a shrill whistle. When everyone falls quiet again, he turns to me and waits.

"Thanks. So. The other stuff that seems to go viral is, like, catchy songs and dances and flash mobs. And we've got the perfect person to be the face of that kind of thing."

I search the faces before me, wondering if he's shown up since I started talking. But even though he's not here, at least three different people all say in unison, "Fernando Montoya."

Then, over the excited chatter, Cole's voice cuts through: "But what's the hashtag?"

I glance at Sol, who nods, and then Will, who gives me a thumbs-up. I wasn't sure they'd get it when I told them. I didn't want it to seem like having a period is an emergency. I wanted the need for support to feel urgent.

I took a deep breath. Then I announced it: "Code Red."

Fernando is in, and Verity and some of her cheer friends are willing to choreograph. Cole's writing parody lyrics and Soledad's scouting locations. This was all decided at the high school at lunch the next day, which Soledad live texted me. I finally had to turn my own phone off during our lunch because Maribel, who had been tentatively friendly for the past week, was getting annoyed and overly curious about my bazillion notifications. I doubted it would go over well if she knew it was her own sister texting me.

The plan is to record the next weekend, giving us a full week to prepare. Those preparations don't really involve me, except the text chain keeps me updated. The dance teacher at the high school is letting them use the dance studio to choreograph and practice.

Soledad has found the perfect spot at Green Lake, where all the flash-mob participants can blend in as joggers and Frisbee throwers and folks sitting on blankets and then suddenly jump up and join in with Fernando's song and dance. If we're lucky, we'll get one of those late-spring days that are gloriously sunny, and absolutely everyone in Seattle heads out to Green Lake to worship the sun. The plan doesn't rely on a large live audience, but those always make flash mobs more fun.

I once saw a video of a flash mob on a crowded New York subway car, where the cast of a Broadway show was scattered throughout, and then suddenly they were singing and dancing (as much as they could) in the aisle. Or another one at this big city park, where out of nowhere people who seemed like they were just passing through whipped out instruments and suddenly there was an impromptu orchestra.

As fun as it would be to participate in a flash mob, I think it might be even more fun to happen upon one as a random passerby.

While we hope random passersby will post their own videos, Micah is our resident videographer, responsible for posting high-quality video labeled with our hashtag, and others that promote menstrual equity.

"Okay," Will says one afternoon as he video calls me from the high school dance studio. "They're about to do a run-through. You have to envision them in dorky eighties neon workout clothes, which they'll cover with normal hoodies and stuff before they start."

He pans his camera phone to Fernando, stretching in the center of the dance floor.

"Say hi to Eden!" Will instructs.

"Hi to Eden!" Fernando calls, shooting the camera his megawatt smile. This is totally going to work.

Off camera, I hear Verity's voice. "Okay, everybody. Places. Ready?" And then the music starts thumping.

When Fernando begins singing, I start to understand why Maribel and Julie are so giggly over the mere thought of him, and why multiple people at Verity's house knew exactly who the star needed to be. Even through Will's shaky video and an unpolished rehearsal, he's incredible, and I want to be a part of whatever his cause is.

Except his cause is my cause!

"Amazing!" I call when the number ends.

"Eden says 'amazing,'" Will reports.

Fernando shrugs, taking a swig of water. "Eh, I messed up the footwork on the bridge, but I'll get it by Saturday."

Suddenly, the phone jolts out of Will's hand and I'm looking at Verity's face. "Eden! When Nando says, 'Free!' and throws his hands up in the air, we want him to be throwing handfuls of pads and tampons."

Envisioning that, I burst out laughing.

"Right?" she says with a grin. "And then, ideally, everyone dancing in the flash mob will have handfuls too that they can throw during the chorus. Some people can bring their own, but we were wondering . . ."

It takes me a second to realize where she's going. "Oh! You want me to supply them?"

"Yes! As many as you can. That would be amazing. And you'll be there on Saturday, right, Eden?"

"I hope so. I'm going to try."

"You have to. I've got a part just for you."

"Oh, no, I don't sing or dance!"

"I'm not going to ask you to sing or dance, I promise."

Well, okay. I guess I can be a background jogger or something. It was all my idea, after all. And while it already feels incredible watching it unfold on camera, I can't even imagine the feeling of being in the middle of it.

"Okay," I say. "I'll be there."

Asking Mom for a donation of products is out. There'd be no way to avoid explaining that it's for a menstrual equity campaign. Which is exactly what she doesn't want me doing.

I grab what I still have under my bathroom sink. My mom's bathroom has more, but she might notice if I take hers. There's a jackpot in the guest bathroom though, and then when I'm looking for a box to hold them all, I find a megajackpot in the garage—an actual case of discontinued tampons that had a typo on the packaging.

I'm pretty sure I can convince my mom to take me to Green Lake tomorrow, but there's no way to sneak these there under her nose. I text Will with my conundrum while I go to figure out what I own that could pass for wacky 80s workout clothes.

A few minutes later Will texts back.

Leave it to me.

Chapter Sixteen

I decided the (partial) truth was my best approach for getting to Green Lake.

I used some electric-pink fabric from Mom's bins to make myself a slouchy cropped T-shirt that falls off one shoulder. Paired with some bright leggings, that's my best attempt at 80s workout gear. I cover both with gray sweats and a black hoodie, and lace on running shoes I haven't worn since before my injury.

"You always used to complain about running," Mom says as I climb into the car. She's agreed to drop me at Green Lake on her way to a meditation retreat.

She's right about running. I hated it when it was for cardio conditioning. All I really wanted to do was fly through the air. "Yeah. But I've been feeling out of shape. Skye's a good motivator."

"She's serious about lacrosse?"

"I mean, she's on a travel team." I don't know what being serious about lacrosse would look like. Shooting for a college scholarship? Training for the Olympics? Is there even lacrosse in the Olympics? I wonder if my mom has ever had a hobby just for the fun of having the hobby. Maybe sewing?

"I'd like to meet her sometime," Mom says as she pulls into one of those drive-through coffee huts. "Maybe we could have her and her parents over for dinner."

"Mom, we're just starting to be friends."

"Well, heaven forbid I be friendly with your friends and their families," she huffs. She rolls down the window and places her order. While we wait, she adds, "I'm sorry. This is new for me, too, you know. For the longest time, everyone you spent time with was from the gym. I know I'm not around a lot, and I believe in continuing to pursue my goals, not despite being a mother but *because* I'm a mother. As an example for you. And to provide you with everything I never had. But not being around as much also means I want to make sure you're spending time with quality people."

And there it is. A rare moment of my mom actually opening up to me, ruined by the implication that Maribel and her family, Will, and Raven aren't "quality people."

I don't say anything as she pulls back out and drives the rest of the way to Green Lake.

"Okay, well, there's Skye," I say as she pulls up in a loading zone across the street from the lake. "Thanks, Mom!"

"Wait, when will you be home?"

"I'm not sure. We might get lunch after?"

"Okay, text me when you're heading home."

"Won't you be meditating?"

"Yes, but I'll meditate better if I know there'll be a communication from you when I sneak away to check my phone." She reaches into her purse and pulls out a couple of twenties. "I don't think the snack bar takes cards," she says. "Treat your friend."

"Thanks."

I don't walk far before Maribel and Julie come running up to me.

"Eden! Hi! I'm so excited!" Maribel says, a super-high ponytail flopping into her face, no hint of the tension between us.

"Hi! I didn't know you'd be here. Hi, Julie."

"Are you kidding?" Julie says. "Fernando came to our rehearsal yesterday, and Dot let him have the last half hour to teach us the choreography. A bunch of the *Joseph* cast is here."

I look around as we reach the snack shop. They blend in with muted clothes over their real costumes, but sure enough, I spot several kids from school, a bunch of the cheerleaders, Raven and some of her friends, and—

"Eden!" Will appears, cheeks flushed with excitement. "Mission accomplished!" He holds up his hands for a double high five.

"What mission?" Maribel asks, suspicious.

Will points to a stack of boxes behind the snack bar. "Eden left our supply of products in her garden shed, and Mom and I swung by after she and her mom had left the house."

Maribel and Julie exchange a look. "Why didn't you bring them yourself?"

That's right. Maribel still doesn't know that I'm not supposed to be hanging out with her or anyone else who wants to make things better.

But I'm saved by Verity, who waves me over to where she stands with a couple of other girls, Fernando, and Micah.

"Sorry," I tell my friends. "I'll be right back."

"Eden, hi! Thanks for the products, that's such a big help. And don't worry, we're going to make sure to pick up any that get left on the ground to stock the bathrooms at school."

"Oh yeah, no problem." (Aside from the fact that I had to pull a total undercover operation to get them here.)

"Okay, so, we wanted to talk to you about your part."

"Really, I don't need to be—"

"Eden." Fernando stops me with a hand on my shoulder, and I swear I can hear Maribel sigh from here. "You must. I won't go on unless you do too."

He can't be serious. Dozens of people didn't work on this all week for him to back out because I've got stage fright.

But Verity takes my moment of hesitation to barrel through. "At the end of the song, it all builds toward this huge finale where Nando's holding this super-long note and everyone around him is throwing products, and there's going to be this awesome musical crescendo, and we'd like to have you come tumbling through the shot, right in front of him."

"Tumbling?"

"That's what they call it, right? Like a gymnastics pass?"

"Oh! I mean . . ."

I haven't tumbled since my injury. The doctors did say when I completed physical therapy that I could still do gymnastics, just not on the punishing training schedule required of elite gymnasts. Still, I'm way out of practice.

I roll out my shoulder. "I don't know."

"It doesn't have to be, like, Olympic level," Verity says. "It could even be a string of cartwheels."

I start to laugh, then realize she's serious. A string of cart-wheels would be enough. I could have done that when I was six. My coaches, my mom, would have been horrified if I'd ever done a string of cartwheels as a tumbling pass. Because why do something if you aren't going to do it at the very highest level?

Maybe for this, right here. Being a part of something, and bringing attention to a cause I believe in.

"Okay. I think I can figure something out. But I need to warm up. How long do I have?"

Cole consults a clipboard, and then their phone. "We're still waiting on a few more people. Could you be ready in ten minutes?"

Ten minutes. Okay, sure. No big deal. I walk away from the others and, after a few paces, make it a jog. Partly to warm my body up and partly to put some distance between me and whoever's here for the flash mob. It's a little hard to tell, since people have camouflaged their 80s clothes. There do seem to an awful lot more super-high ponytails than normal on the folks at Green Lake today.

"You're going the wrong direction," says a voice, and then Skye falls in step with me.

I explain my mission, and even though I didn't want eyes on me, somehow it feels comfortable to have Skye, another athlete, helping me warm up.

"I didn't know you were coming," I say as we do burpees.

"Julie invited me," she says. "I hardly get to see her anymore."

"I know, they're so busy with the show!"

"Yeah, and I'm busy with lacrosse," she says, transitioning into knee lifts. "It's a little weird, we've been best friends since forever, but lately we seem to be interested in different things. But I still care about her! And miss her, even." She looks at me with wide eyes. "Don't tell her I said anything?"

"Of course not." And I get it. I mean, Maribel and I haven't been friends for that long. But we shared this intense bond when everything went down with Graham, and I thought maybe I was going to have my first real BFF. Then it turned out that we have pretty different interests. I still really like Maribel, and want to be her friend. But the truth is, I have more in common with Skye. And Will.

"Okay, no more stalling," Skye says, glancing at her watch. "Let's see some flips."

I start with cartwheels and feel only a tiny twinge in my shoulder. Which, to be fair, might be because I was tensing up, preparing for pain. I take a breath, roll my shoulder out, and do three back handsprings. No twinge.

"Nice!" Skye says.

"Thanks."

I play around with a few flips and roundoffs, and decide on a roundoff back handspring Arabian, which earns a cheer from Skye when I try it out.

"You feel ready?" she asks.

"Yep."

She glances at her phone as we walk back toward the snack shop. "Okay, when we're in place, Cole will send out a final text to alert everyone that it's go time."

My place is over by the Bathhouse (which is actually a theater, but it used to be the changing rooms for swimmers at the lake and the name stuck). The first part of the song and dance will start closer to the snack shed, but it'll move along the path toward me, and then I'll do my flips during the last, long, sustained note.

At least those are my instructions. We'll see how it works out.

My phone buzzes with a text. Go time, Cole says.

A moment later a booming electric guitar starts things off. A high school guy stands next to an amp wearing a bright green sweatband and wrist bands. Passersby give him curious looks, because live music at Green Lake is not the norm, but they keep walking. Then a group of cheer girls shed their hoodies and start freestyle rocking out to the music in neon workout gear. A few people stop to watch, but it's still small enough that it could be a spontaneous dance party.

Then Fernando jumps onto a park bench, spreads his arms wide, and begins to sing. He's wearing knee socks and silky running shorts, a tank top over a T-shirt, plus sweatbands on his head and wrists, and each garment is a different neon color.

Now everyone in the area is watching.

"Baby, the time has come," his rich voice projects across the open park. "Your lining's on the run. You can't find a single tampon inside that disgusting machine at school!"

Now phones are out, recording. Fernando jumps off the bench as he's joined by not only the cheer girls but about a dozen middle schoolers, including Maribel, Julie, and Skye. They must have completely depleted the area thrift stores of every single piece of neon spandex in stock. Not to mention hair spray—everyone's do's are mile high.

"But now I've got what you need," he sings, handing the first pad to Will, who beams in a T-shirt that says *Fame*, from the movie the song Fernando is singing is from. "Protection guaranteed! I've got all the tampons you want"—Maribel catches a tampon she'll probably never use but keep in a shrine to Fernando Montoya for the rest of her life—"Also pads, if you like. Don't you think they should be . . ."

And here's the big moment. At some point in the last couple of lines, someone has filled Fernando's hands with dozens of products.

"FREE!" he shouts as he throws his arms up and showers menstrual products all over, along with all the dancers, who then break into a choreographed dance with him.

"In every school and shelter!" they belt. "Clinics and libraries too!" Then, as they all yell "Whoo!" everyone throws products. "Community health centers, government offices now. Wow!" Again, on "wow," more pads go flying. "Paid for by corporations, with plenty of money to spare. Fair! I wanna help my neighbor with basic essential needs!"

Then more people come out of the woodwork—I mean literally, emerging from the trees—chanting and stepping in time behind Fernando, "Always free, always free, always free, always free."

Fernando continues for another verse, as more and more onlookers gather around. It's an incredible performance, no doubt, and it's also an incredible visual. There are at least fifty dancers in wild neon costumes, and the pads and tampons keep flying.

Then he's at the chorus again, belting, "Don't you think they should be . . . FREE?!"

Another group—I didn't know there could possibly be more—joins in, including drama teacher Dot and our school librarian. I've figured out the chorus, so I'm singing along, even though no one's paying attention to me. "In every school and shelter," we sing, and my phone buzzes in my pocket, letting me know that at the end of this chorus, it's my turn. I roll out my shoulders and breathe deeply. How am I this nervous for a simple tumbling pass? The day has already been a huge success, whether or not I pull it off.

"Paid for by corporations," everyone sings, drawing closer. "With plenty of money to spare (fair!)."

Then it's my personal go time. Fernando steps up onto the spot where I was told he'd stop, hitting his mark perfectly, and as he begins that long, sustained note, I go.

It's like I'm back on a floor routine in competition, except for the part where I'm tumbling across grass with way more potential obstacles. But the dancers have been warned to clear the way, so I focus on maintaining my form and remaining loose (except where I have to remain tightly controlled—it's a balance).

Before I know it, I'm done. Fernando times it perfectly, finishing his note as I stick my landing and the gathered crowd explodes in cheers and applause.

It's an exhilaration that's familiar but also unlike anything I've ever felt before. I've hit much harder routines, with much higher stakes. Nailing a routine might mean moving forward in a competition, or even winning. Just now I'm feeling the same rush, even though there's no medal at stake. And even though we have an important cause, it's not like my tumbling pass is going to be the thing that ends period poverty for anyone.

But my heart's still pounding, and I feel like I could keep doing flips all the way around the lake. I grab some tampons at my feet and throw them to the gathered crowd, shouting, "Free!"

Fernando gives me a double high five on his way to jump up on another park bench.

"Thanks so much for your attention, folks!" he calls. "We're raising awareness for menstrual equity and trying to get an initiative on the ballot that would finance the already required free menstrual products in schools, as well as offer them in other public places like libraries and free clinics! If you're posting on social media, please use the hashtag Code Red, and if you're a registered voter, please see someone with a clipboard"—he points out the cheer squad spread out with clipboards—"and give us your autograph. If you'd like to help us out, we're accepting volunteers!"

With that, he hops off the bench and comes straight over to me. "Nice job, Suni Lee," he says. "Perfect landing."

"Thanks!" I'm giddy, and not because he's swoony Fernando Montoya, but because he's awesome, and I'm awesome, and together with all these other people, we're doing something awesome.

Then Will's throwing his arms around me. "That rocked!"

"I know!" I laugh as I hug him back.

I don't see Maribel and my other friends in the crowd, but Soledad catches my eye and waves us over. She's huddled with Cole and Micah, and all three of them are on their phones.

"Cole's going to take a little time to make sure we've got a high-quality edit to post," Soledad explains.

"But people are already starting to post their own videos." Cole holds up their screen to show us.

"Are they using the hashtag?" Will asks.

"Hashtag Code Red," Micah says, holding up his phone to show another video from a different perspective.

"Even with the dancers who were here today, we have a ton of new people who want to help petition," Soledad says.

"That's awesome!"

Soledad is pulled away then, and Maribel finds us, bubbling over with excitement. "That was so cool," she says. "Fernando was amazing!"

"You were too," Skye says as she joins us. "How's the shoulder?"

"Oh. It's fine." I've been on such a high, I haven't even thought about it, which is kind of incredible.

"Hi, are you Will?" Julie goes straight up to Will. "I'm Julie. I've heard all about you, and it's time we met."

Will blinks at her. "Yes, hi. You're playing the Narrator in *Joseph*, right?"

Julie beams. "Yes. Are you coming to the show?"

Will glances at me. "I mean, yeah. Of course."

Maribel and Julie start telling us everything about the show, which goes into tech on Tuesday and opens next weekend. I'm listening, sort of, but mostly I'm looking around at all these people who came out to participate in this thing that was my idea. That might make a difference in the world. And it feels kind of great.

Chapter Seventeen

Everyone takes a couple of days off, but on Tuesday there's a team meeting at Soledad's house. I get home just in time, after staying late at school to help Dot with all the final costume issues.

Mom's still fine with me working on the show, and has even bought tickets to see it on Friday night. As soon as I'm home from tech rehearsal, I grab an apple and head up to the attic. "I've got homework," I tell her as I pass through.

But what I'm really going to do is get on a video call to participate remotely in the meeting debriefing the flash mob. Will answers on the first ring and pans me around to see who's there— Soledad, Fernando, Micah, Cole, Verity, and the kid who played the electric guitar.

"Hi, Eden!" Everyone waves.

"How's our fearless leader?" Fernando says.

"I don't know. Ask Soledad," I say, and everyone laughs.

Soledad takes that as her cue. "Okay, so the response to the flash mob has been amazing. We signed up twenty-three new volunteers for petitioning around the Seattle area, and Verity is making up a schedule for that. We got inquiries into how people could make donations to support our cause, and I'm meeting with Raven tomorrow afternoon to discuss how we should handle that. And, finally, Micah's going to give us a social media report."

Everyone turns to Micah, whose face looks the same way it pretty much always does. I think he'd have that same unfazed expression whether he just won the lottery or found out his dog died. It's basically impossible to predict how this is going to go. Except that Soledad is twitching with what I think (hope?) is excitement.

Micah pushes his glasses up his nose as he looks down at his tablet. "Social engagement has been very good. Three point two thousand retweets, lots of activity on the hashtag. But we've really taken off on TikTok, where we've gotten almost two hundred thousand likes."

Soledad is beaming and Fernando looks pretty pleased. "This is great," Verity says. "But how does it all translate into support for the cause?"

"That's the best part!" Soledad exclaims, unable to wait for Micah to spit it out. "Across platforms, we've received more than a hundred messages from people across the state who want to petition!"

"That's huge!" Verity says.

"Right? So far we've got people in Tacoma, Spokane, Yakima, Bellingham, and Olympia. And those people are all going to build their own teams in their areas!"

"Go Team Code Red!" Will hollers, and then drops his phone in all the excitement. "Sorry," he says when he gets it back in his hands. He grins sheepishly at me. The others celebrate in the background, but all I see is Will's face, and his huge smile. "This is so amazing, Eden. Can you believe it?"

I could hardly believe it when I learned that people all over the state would be working to gather signatures for us. But even harder to believe is the next day, when Dot pulls me out of math class.

She looks so serious when she pokes her head in and asks Mr. Knabb if she can borrow me for a minute. I can't figure out what kind of costume catastrophe would require my emergency assistance.

But as soon as I step into the hall, her face changes to utter and complete glee. I have to jog to keep up with her as she races to the drama room and into her tiny office.

"What is going on, Dot?"

She plunks me down in her desk chair and presses play on her computer. It takes me a second to register what I'm seeing. On the left is our flash-mob video, with Fernando singing his heart out. But on the right is a young woman in what looks like a bathroom, singing along and harmonizing with Fernando like they were made to sing together. Her voice is gorgeous, and every time they sing "Free!" she throws pads around her room too.

"That's hilarious," I say. "Her voice is amazing."

Dot reaches out and pauses the video. "Wait, do you not know who that is?"

I'm struck by the feeling I had so many times during my gymnastics years. Kids at school would be talking about the latest movie or celebrity or meme or trend, and I'd have no idea what they were talking about because I never had time for anything except gymnastics.

Except now, instead of feeling like I'm not as cool as a group of my peers, I'm feeling like I'm not as cool as Dot, with her rhinestone glasses and white hair. (To be fair, Dot is pretty cool.)

"Um . . . no?"

But I look closer, and right as it's dawning on me why the girl looks familiar, Dot squeals, "That's Madison Cho!!!"

Even I, totally out of touch that I am, know who Madison Cho is. And not only because Russell's floor routine was set to an instrumental version of one of her songs.

"She's got a ton of Grammys!" Dot says. "Been on tons of magazine covers! She's going to play Éponine in *Les Mis* in the fall!"

"Yeah, of course, I—"

"Now listen." Dot hushes me and presses play again, right in time for the last line, Fernando's sustained note and my tumbling pass, and all throughout that long, last note, Madison goes on a stunning vocal run, her voice rising and falling and practically harmonizing with herself.

But her video doesn't stop when ours does. She talks straight to the camera. "This is an amazing cause, y'all. Period products should be free, and they definitely shouldn't be a reason girls—sorry, *menstruators*, I'm still learning—can't get the education they deserve. I am one hundred percent in support of this, and any of y'all in Washington State should get in touch to help them get this thing on the ballot! Details below!"

I can't move. I can't even think. How is this happening?

"Look at the likes," Dot says. "Look at the shares! I wonder if Fernando's seen?"

Fernando has definitely seen. By lunchtime our text chain has more notifications than it's had in the past month. Soledad is calling an emergency team meeting after school, though I don't know what there is to meet about. Maybe how to handle all the new volunteers?

You have to be there, Eden, she writes. I'll deal with your mother myself if I need to.

The meeting is at Casa Esperanza, which is less than ideal for me if Mom suddenly decides to check on my whereabouts, but Soledad mysteriously said it needed to be there.

Raven drops off Will and me at the same time Fernando pulls into the lot with Verity, Cole, and Micah. We find Soledad in the office, looking triumphant.

"Finally!" Soledad says, even though my school let out less than ten minutes ago. "Sit down, everyone, sit down!"

While we're situating ourselves, Flor runs into the room, waving what looks like a pair of princess underwear on a stick like a flag, and yelling, "You're going to be on TV! You're going to be on TV!"

Wait, what?

Soledad rolls her eyes, but not even Flor stealing her thunder can get her down.

"Okay, yes, the little tyrant is correct. We're going to be on TV!"

She explains that when they saw the Madison Cho video, her adviser suggested they contact local media to get some more attention on the cause.

I'm honestly not sure how much more attention we can take.

"So they're going to be here in"—she checks her watch—"twenty minutes."

"Who?" Verity asks.

"KIRO!"

"TV?" Fernando asks.

"Yep!"

Sol's organized us all here at Casa Esperanza with ulterior motives. "I figured this way we can tell people who're just learning about menstrual equity how helpful it can be to donate supplies to food banks."

This is all moving so much faster than I ever could have dreamed. But it's okay, I keep telling myself. The cause is the point. I can stay out of it—

"The reporter said she could talk to two of us. It's going to be a short segment, and too many people in a story like this is confusing or something. I think it should be Fernando and Eden."

My head snaps up. "What?"

"Not me," Fernando says. "I'm already in the video. It's your senior project, Sol."

"I agree," Verity says.

"All in favor of Sol and Eden?" Will says, shooting his hands up. Everyone else puts their hands up too. Except me.

"Okay," Soledad says. "I'm thinking the best place to shoot—"

"Wait. I don't . . . . It can't be me."

"What are you talking about?" Will says. "It has to be you. The whole thing was your idea."

"No, I can't—"

"Look." Fernando leans forward across the table and pins me

with his gaze. "I get stage fright, I honestly do. But you've got this. You're articulate and funny and you believe in this cause."

"It's not that! I'm not supposed to be here. My mom doesn't want me . . . She told me I couldn't. . . ."

"I'll talk to your mom," Silvia says. "She's going to be proud of you—"

"No, don't, please! You'll make it worse! It's you! It's all of you! You're a bad influence. She doesn't want me spending time with you!"

For some reason I deliver that last part to Will, and the hurt in his eyes is more than I can bear. I run from the room.

I'm not going to call a car and then stand there in the parking lot waiting. I'd probably be there when the news van drove up or, worse, when everyone else came outside to meet them. So I start walking north. Aurora Avenue is loud and busy, lined with seedy hotels and pot stores and the occasional coffee shop. After weeks of feeling stuck at home, now that's the only place I want to be.

I pull out my phone. If I call a car, my mom will see the notification that I ordered a ride from a random spot on Aurora, close to Casa Esperanza.

Maybe I can walk all the way home.

But I'm standing at a crosswalk, waiting for the light to tell me to go, when Fernando's car pulls up beside me.

"Get in!" he hollers. Only, it's not Fernando. It's Micah. "Fernando's doing the interview with Soledad," he says. "Where to?"

I direct him toward my house. Who sent him to pick me up? I can't imagine Micah would have thought of it himself. Raven could have come, but she didn't. Maybe she and Will are too upset by what I said.

I don't ask. Micah's quiet, and I might burst into tears if I try to talk about what just happened. So I give him the directions to get me home. Then I run upstairs, curl myself around Blizz on my bed, and cry.

Chapter Eighteen

The next morning I stay home from school. Mom's gone when I get up anyway, so I text her that I woke up with a sore throat and go back to sleep.

By ten I can't laze around in bed any longer. My stomach is growling and my throat actually is kind of sore. I make my way downstairs, grateful it's not an Olga day. I let Blizz out and I'm searching for something breakfast-like when I get a text from Grandma.

You're on the tube, sugar!

I'm on the tube? I cannot be on the tube. I threw a grenade into all my amazing new friendships just so I *wouldn't* be on the tube. I stumble into the living room and turn on the TV, finding KIRO just in time to see the reporter standing next to Soledad and Fernando, and saying, "Back to you, Tom!"

My phone rings with a call from Grandma, but I ignore it, racing back up to the attic to find the station's website and locate the story clip. It's not hard—it's right at the top and already has a ton of views. I hit play, dread bubbling in my stomach.

"I'm here in Shoreline at Casa Esperanza, a full-service food bank and community center serving the lower-income folks of North Aurora," the reporter chirps, standing in front of the building with a clear view of the sign on the window. "I'm with two local high school students"—the camera pans wider to show Soledad and Fernando, looking totally comfortable—"who are working on an exciting ballot initiative!

"This is Soledad Miller-Paz, who's made this her senior project at Shorewood High School. Soledad, can you tell us about the initiative?"

Soledad explains how the high cost of menstrual products can be really difficult for low-income menstruators, causing work or school performance to suffer, and that the problem is even worse for unhoused people.

"And are menstrual products easily found at places like this food bank behind us?" the reporter asks.

"Unfortunately, no. They're rarely donated. Ideally, we could find a solution that wouldn't require people to get their essential needs met by nonprofits."

The reporter turns back to the camera. "So these young people have crafted an initiative to put on the ballot. And, yes, that's legal—Ms. Miller-Paz is eighteen years old and a registered Washington State voter. To get more attention on the cause, they took exactly the approach you might expect from a group of teens—they made a viral video!"

She turns to Fernando. "And here is the star! Tell us about the video, and your unexpected duet!"

Fernando turns his charms on her and the viewing audience, explaining the flash mob and Madison Cho's TikTok support.

"To see the whole video," the reporter says as the camera closes in on her, "search the hashtag Code Red on just about any social media platform. But for now, here's a sneak peek!"

The screen fills with the final chorus of the flash mob as Fernando and dozens of 80s dancers fling menstrual products all over Green Lake and then—there it is—I'm flipping through the picture with the tumbling pass, fast enough that you never see my face, until I stick the landing and the camera is on me for a second before going back to a wide shot.

The longest second ever.

Mom doesn't watch local news. That's what I keep telling myself. She's way too busy for that. She has assistants who brief her on the important economic and political events that could impact MySecret's bottom line, and she doesn't have time for anything as trivial as human-interest stories about a high school student's senior project.

My phone is silent all day.

I start a text to Will about a dozen times, but I delete it every time. It doesn't even matter that I can't text Maribel. I'm sure she's heard from Sol and Silvia what I said and never wants to talk to me again.

Even Blizz doesn't want anything to do with me. For once he's curled up on the couch and doesn't seem to care what I'm up to. Right when I could have used his comforting presence.

If I wasn't sick when I stayed home this morning, I am by the end of the day, after moping around the house, thinking of all the ways I've messed up over the past couple of months. When Mom pulls in, I'm determined to eat whatever takeout food she's brought home, agree with whatever she says, and at least avoid alienating her.

Except she hasn't brought any food, and she's not there for a nice, cordial dinner.

"Did you think I wouldn't find out about this?" is the first thing she says when she walks in.

I know before I look at her outstretched phone that she's seen the video.

"It's not what you—"

"It's not what I think? Let me tell you what I think." She sits at the opposite side of the kitchen table and leans toward me, her eyes steely. Suddenly, I know exactly how she became a Forbes Rising Business Star at thirty-two. "I think I specifically told you I didn't want you hanging out with these people and getting involved in their absurd politics."

"They're not—"

"I'm talking now. I think that not only did you disregard my wishes but you've been sneaking around for months, not only hanging out with them, but actively participating in their political schemes—"

"They didn't—"

"Targeting my own business," she goes on, raising her voice in a way she almost never does, "as some kind of twisted rebellion, or because you truly believe that I'm so evil, I want poor people to suffer."

"I don't think—"

"At this point, I don't honestly care what you think. I've been in meetings all day. The optics on this are a nightmare. It's not the initiative, which we'll flatten if it even gets on the ballot. It's how it looks for the daughter of MySecret's CEO to spearhead a campaign targeting the business her mother worked tooth and nail to build from nothing. A business that includes all kinds of female-empowerment programs, by the way, but that you're making look like capitalist monsters.

"And don't tell me you didn't spearhead it, because Silvia was the first person I called. I know everything."

There's nothing to say, and I don't dare open my mouth because my throat is already tightening and the tears are coming, so all I can hope is to get out of here before that happens.

"You thought you were grounded before?" she says. "This time you're seriously grounded. Nowhere but school and back for the rest of the year. I'll send a car to pick you up, and yes, I will be checking your whereabouts on your phone. Are we clear?"

I nod and hold back my tears until she's left the room, Blizz following after her. The traitor. It's not until I reach my own room that I realize I'm going to miss the opening night of *Joseph and the Amazing Technicolor Dreamcoat*.

Chapter Nineteen

There's no staying home sick the next day, even though this time I genuinely feel awful. I didn't sleep all night. Around two a.m., I sent a text to Will, which I totally regret now, and he still hasn't answered.

But Mom's home when I get up and she takes me to school, staying at the curb to watch until I've walked into the building. We're early, because she needed to get to a video call with the East Coast. So I make my way to the drama room. I don't even expect to find anyone; I just need a quiet place to sit and hide until I can escape into the monotony of classes.

But Dot's there, looking extra frazzled.

"You're early," I say as I dump my backpack on the risers.

"It's the day of the show!" She's a flurry of activity and I'm not even sure how to help. "What's your excuse?"

"My mom had to get to work early."

She nods. "There's a stack of programs on my desk that need

to be folded."

Glad to have something to do, I retrieve them and sit cross-legged on the floor, using the first riser as my surface for making careful folds.

Dot hauls out a cumbersome machine as tall as she is, that looks like some sort of vacuum. She plugs it in. Then she pulls one of the costumes from the rack and hangs it on a hook at the top of the machine.

"It's a steamer," she explains, picking up the vacuumy part of it and aiming it a few inches away from the costumes, moving slowly up and down as a stream of steam flows from it. "It's like an industrial iron. When you're done there, I'll show you how to use it."

There are so many things that happen behind the scenes of a show that I've never even considered when I've sat in the audience. I only see the final result. Sort of like the people who watch a gymnastics competition, and the decade or more of work that has gone into it is boiled down for the viewer into one three-second vault.

Or sort of like running a massive company like MySecret.

"Congratulations on the TV coverage for the initiative," Dot says, hanging the steamed costume on an empty rack and pulling another to get the same treatment. "I was surprised they didn't interview you. Wasn't it your idea?"

"It's Sol's project. And Fernando's the face of it."

Dot frowns. "That doesn't sound like Fernando to me. He's a star, no doubt, but he likes nothing better than sharing the spotlight."

I don't know what it is about Dot that makes me want to tell her everything. Or maybe it's that I'm desperate to talk to someone and everyone else is mad at me.

So I do. I tell her everything, starting with Graham—"If that boy doesn't see some consequences for his actions soon, it'll be too late for him," she mutters darkly—and then explaining about Maribel and Silvia and Casa Esperanza, and Raven and Will, and Mom telling me I couldn't see them anymore, but me sneaking around and the virtual meetings and the flash mob, and finally the horrible moment when I told the people who've been nothing but kind and encouraging and supportive that my mom thinks they're a bad influence.

"And now I can't even go to opening night!" I blubber, my head in my hands.

Dot leaves the steamer and costumes and sits next to me on the riser.

"You've had a rough couple of months," she says.

"Not really! I mean, yeah. But also I've met the coolest people and made some friendships I thought might really last, and learned about problems in the world and worked on fixing them, but now . . ."

"Now what?" she asks gently. "What's the next step?"

"I don't know! I'm sure none of them wants to talk to me again."

"Eden, I think there's an important distinction between what your mom believes about your new friends, and what you believe. You didn't tell them that *you* don't want to hang out with them. You told them your mother doesn't want you hanging out with them."

"But that's awful, isn't it?"

She's thoughtful for a minute. "I bet it hurt some feelings, yes. But when they think about it, you were going out of your way and risking punishment because, despite what your mom believed, you wanted to be with them that much.

"Not that I'm condoning breaking your mother's rules. But at the same time, this is the stage of life you're in. Starting to figure out what your own beliefs are, and sometimes—often—they're different from your parents' beliefs. Figuring out how to navigate that is kind of the whole thing about growing up."

She pats my knee and hauls herself back to her feet with a groan.

"So what do I do now?"

"I think you know," she says.

At lunch I ask Maribel if I can speak to her privately. She's definitely heard about my outburst, because she's very subdued, but she agrees and we walk out to a bench by the basketball court.

"So, um." I shift on the bench, uncomfortable. Suddenly, I'm hyperaware of how close I'm sitting to her. Is it too close? Too far? How awkward can I be?

She waits. Leaving silence unfilled is super not like Maribel.

Eventually, I blurt, "I guess you heard about what I said at Casa Esperanza."

"That we're not good enough for you?"

"No!" I take a breath. "No, that's definitely not what I said. And it's even more definitely not what I think. It's my mom. . . . She doesn't want me hanging out with you. Not only you—your family and Raven and Will."

"That doesn't make it better."

"I know," I hurry to say. "I've just . . . I've been sneaking around, ignoring her wishes, because it matters to me. You matter to me."

"Your initiative matters to you."

"That too. Just like the show matters to you." She nods, giving me that point. "But you've got to know how much you and everything you've introduced me to has meant. You've opened up my entire world."

"Glad we could help teach you that not everyone lives in a mansion."

Ouch. That's not what I meant. But maybe it's what it seemed like, to Maribel and everyone else. "It's true that I've learned more about what poverty looks like," I say carefully. "But I've also learned about doing things because they matter, and not because they'll earn me gold stars. I've learned to keep extra pads in my bag in case someone needs them. I've learned I can sew, and that theater is really cool."

That gets a small smile out of her.

"I've learned—I'm still learning—how to have friends. Real friends. Not people-I-see-every-day-at-the-gym-but-don't-really-know friends. And I'm still messing that up, but I am trying."

She gives me a tiny smile. She's messed up too, but I know she's also trying. "So what now?"

I sigh. "I don't know. I mean, obviously, we can still see each other at school. But I'm totally grounded and my mom's going to be monitoring me really closely."

"What about the show tonight?"

I shake my head.

"Wait, what? No, I'm sorry." Maribel stands, all hints of a smile erased from her face. "You cared enough to sneak around for meetings with my sister and her friends. To go star in a viral video, to gather signatures. If I'm really supposed to believe you care about me as a friend, you'll find a way to get to the show tonight."

It's too much to hope my mom will have an evening meeting. No, she's cleared her schedule in order to play jailer. And while I'm not actually confined to the attic, that's where I'm staying for now. Until I figure out how to escape.

But even if I could get past my mom, I'm not sure how I'd get to the school. Will still hasn't replied to my texts, so I definitely can't ask Raven to pick me up. If I call a car, Mom will know.

The only option is to take the bus. Which isn't a big deal in the day. But it'll definitely be dark by the time the show gets out. The bus is one thing, but our windy street with no sidewalk is another.

If I'm really supposed to believe you care about me as a friend, you'll find a way to get to the show tonight.

I can't even begin to imagine my mom's rage when she finds out I've snuck out. But at this point, I don't see how things can get any worse. And I don't know, maybe this is weird, but part of me feels like at least she's showing that she cares about me, in her own twisted way. Or maybe there's the tiniest chance I'll be able to sneak out and back in and she won't even know. She'll still be as furious as she is now, but I'll have shown Maribel I care.

Maybe I'll even have a chance to make things right with the other people I've hurt.

I go downstairs and pick a fight as quickly as I possibly can. It's not hard.

"I brought home Thai," Mom says calmly from the kitchen table, where she's working on her computer.

"No thanks," I say in my snottiest voice possible.

"Just because you're grounded doesn't mean we can't eat together like normal."

"Like normal? Normal is me eating by myself while you're off having important meetings and dinners in fancy restaurants."

Mom actually jerks her head back like I slapped her. I'm being snotty on purpose, except it also kind of feels good to say these things I've felt for so long.

"Eden, I—"

"Spare me the speech about how you're giving me the life you never got. We both know this is all for you, not me."

I grab a box of crackers and an apple. "And leave me alone. In case you couldn't tell, I can't stand the sight of you."

I'm shaking when I get back to my room. I've never spoken to my mom like that. And it was true, the first part—she leaves me alone too much, always trying to be more and more successful, make more and more money. But I don't really believe it's all for her. It's at least as much for me as it is for her.

But I have a lifetime ahead of me to mend things with Mom. If I don't show up for Maribel tonight, I've lost her forever. Not only her but the whole constellation of wonderful people she's introduced me to. I'll be back to spending my days alone, with no purpose, no reason to care about anything.

Getting out of the house is a lot easier than it seems in teen movies where they have to climb out windows and scale trellises or drainpipes or oak trees. I gather my things, wait until Mom takes her food and encloses herself in her room, her sanctuary, like I know she will, and slip out the front door.

I do arrange pillows under my blankets to look like I'm in bed and leave a fashion design competition streaming on my computer, but I doubt she'll even venture up to the attic tonight. Or if she does, I'll be long gone.

I keep my phone flashlight on as I make my way through the windy roads out to the main one, where I can catch the bus. It's weird how a road you go down five days a week can seem so much creepier when you're not supposed to be on it. The looming trees make it feel darker than it really is, and a passing tabby cat makes my heart leap out of my chest.

I give up trying to act brave and mature and run to the main road. I'm standing at a bus stop in the dark alone (have I mentioned I'm alone?) for longer than I'd like, nervous now that I'm not only going to be mugged but also that I'm going to be late to the show, and I'm not even sure which is worse.

But I get onto the bus and sit right behind the driver, where the harsh fluorescent lights are weirdly comforting. I make it to the school just in time to grab a seat in the back as the lights are going down.

The show is amazing. Julie has an impressive voice; she's our guide through the wild story, and each musical number is a different style.

The costumes look incredible, if I do say so.

Pharaoh isn't in the first act, but Maribel plays various ensemble roles. I don't think she can possibly see me, all the way in the back. But my eyes never leave her when she's on the stage.

Finally, it's intermission. As people stand and stretch and file out to buy candy in the lobby, I see them. Everyone I need to talk to, all in one place. Raven and Will, who doesn't meet my eye, Silvia and Soledad, and even Fernando, the only one who gives me a grin and a wave when he sees me, like he has no clue about all the relationships at stake tonight.

"Eden!"

Turns out there is one other person who's glad to see me. Flor darts into my aisle and throws her arms around me. "I haven't seen you in a million zillion years!"

"Hi, Chrysanthemum."

She wrinkles her nose. "It's Amaryllis now. Try to keep up."

Silvia follows her into the aisle as people continue to stream past her to the lobby. "Hi, Eden."

Flor's eyes alight on the mini Rubik's Cube dangling off my bag. "Want to play with that?" I ask her, detaching it. "Hi, Silvia." I step over Flor as she hunches over the puzzle cube. "I am so, so sorry about what happened at Casa Esperanza."

Her eyes are kind. "I am too."

I don't know what she's sorry about, but I go on, "I want you to know the past couple of months getting to know you and your family and your work have changed my life."

"I'm so glad."

"I don't want you to think that what my mom thinks or believes has anything to do with me."

She smiles. "Of course I know that. And so does Maribel. And Sol. No one is upset with you."

I blink at her in disbelief.

"Eden, we are not our parents. And Maribel would tell you that's a very good thing. Of course it hurts to think someone might not approve of who we are, when we feel like we're doing our best—"

"You are!"

"But that's about your mom's beliefs. You were only trying—and failing, sometimes—to figure out where you stand in all of it."

I feel like I might burst into tears, which is weird when I should be feeling so relieved. I *am* feeling so relieved. "Sol's not mad at me either? She took me off the text chain."

Silvia smiles and squeezes me arm. "Sol's not mad. She didn't want you to feel left out by seeing all the conversations about things you couldn't be a part of."

Oh. "And Will?"

Silvia hesitates. "You should talk to Will," she finally says. "Florcita, ven. We've got to go if we're going to get to the bathroom before intermission is over."

Flor looks up with big eyes. "I haven't Rubixed the cube yet!"

"You can take it," I tell her. "Amaryllis." In an instant, her tear-filled eyes light up and she scrambles after her mom.

I follow after them too, before I lose my nerve. At first I don't see Will in the crowd, but then I catch a glimpse of his hair through the window. I make my way outside and find him sitting on a bench, alone.

"Hey," I say. He flinches at the sound of my voice. "Can I sit?"

"I can't stop you," he says, his voice flat.

"Will, I am so, so sorry about what I said."

"What part?"

This is clearly not going to be as easy as it was with Silvia and Maribel.

"Everything I said at Casa Esperanza, that was about my mom, her rules and what she wants for me. It had nothing to do with what I think."

"But you still wouldn't stand up to her and put your face on the project."

"I was standing up to her every time I met up with you guys!

And being in the flash mob. And being here right now."

He shrugs.

"I'm sorry," I say again. "I'm not sure what else to say. Maribel understood. . . ."

"Yeah, well, it's different for Maribel, isn't it?"

Is it? Is it different because Will and I got closer than Maribel and I did?

"I'm not sure I understand."

"Obviously."

"Will, please. I'm trying. I snuck out of my house while grounded so I could be here and make this right. Please talk to me."

"Fine." He shifts on the bench so his body is facing mine. "Maribel's got no shortage of people loving her and supporting her and forgiving her when she's flighty or selfish and giving her endless chances."

"But you have Raven—"

"I do, and she's got me, and we're the only people in the world who we both know we can rely on one hundred percent. We're different. We know we're different. I'm different. And someone 'not approving' of me hurts more than you might think."

"Oh, Will. That has nothing to do with what my mom thinks. I don't think she even knows . . . how you're different. It's the activism and the politics part of it all."

"I am political," he says. "Just by existing."

A bell chimes and some lights flicker, indicating that we need to go back inside for the second act. He stands.

"Will." I stand too and grab his hand. We both stare at it. "Sorry, is this okay?"

I start to let go, but Will holds on tighter. "Will you at least let me try to earn back your trust?"

Finally, he nods, then drops my hand and walks away.

The second act is incredible, and it's Maribel's time to shine. Her sparkly white jumpsuit (which I hemmed) fits perfectly, and her hair is all poufed up to suggest Elvis, while still being perfectly Maribel.

She's hilarious, and the audience agrees. Fernando starts a standing ovation after her biggest number, and it's a testament to Maribel's stage presence that she doesn't swoon right there.

Finally, the show is over and the actors stream off the stage in their costumes to greet their friends and family.

I make my way toward the group crowded around Maribel but hang back while her sisters give her flowers and her parents take pictures.

Raven gives her a big hug, and Will does too. He and Maribel exchange words and both glance over at me. I give an awkward wave.

Maribel drags Will with her and throws her arms around me. "You came!"

"Of course I came. You were amazing!"

"Thank you! I love my costume!"

"We're going out for ice cream," Maribel's dad says as the theater empties out. "Want to come?"

I glance at Raven, who looks stiff, and Will, who doesn't meet my eye.

"No, I've got to get home." I've pushed my luck enough. If I get in without Mom realizing I was gone, it will be a teen movie miracle. With the entire Miller-Paz family piling into one car, I know they don't have space for me anyway, and I'm not asking Raven for a ride.

"Want us to wait until your mom gets here?" Silvia asks as we head out to the parking lot, where she assumes I'm getting picked up.

"No thanks." I wave at the theater, which is all still lit up. "Dot's still around."

"Okay, sweetheart. You're still welcome with us anytime, when you get things sorted with your mom."

I wait until both cars have left the lot, and then I begin walking toward the bus stop.

Chapter Twenty

I don't get far before a car slows down next to me. My heart races and I reach for my phone. We're on a busy street, but still.

"Hey, Eden!"

The tension whooshes out of me as I recognize Fernando's voice and turn to see his familiar blue car. "Need a ride?"

"That would be amazing."

"Bit late for walking home alone," he observes after I tell him what direction to head.

"It was the only way I could see the show," I explain.

"And what a great show it was, huh?"

"Yeah. You played Pharaoh, right?"

"How'd you know that?"

I tell him about the framed photo on Dot's wall, and then Fernando's off, telling me way-back stories about Dot when he was in middle school. Passing a gas station about halfway to my house, he pulls in. "Do you mind?"

"No, of course not."

Fernando jumps out of the car and pays for the gas at the pump, inserting the hose into his car. Then he leans in the window. "Hey, I'm going to say hi to some buddies while it pumps. I'll be back in a minute."

He lopes across the parking lot to where a few guys are seated in the back of a pickup. I don't recognize any of them from the flash mob or the meeting at Verity's house.

But I hear them as they laugh loudly and greet Fernando. A few minutes pass and the car jolts when the gas stops pumping. Fernando doesn't return. It's fine. By driving me, he'll get me home much faster than I would have on the bus, even if he talks with his buddies for a few more minutes.

Except a few minutes turn into ten. The next time I turn around to see if he's headed back, I notice something else instead—one of his buddies hands Fernando a can of beer, and he takes a long swig.

Everything good that happened tonight turns into a lead ball in my stomach.

I pull out my phone. There's a takeoff text from Dad. A text from Maribel using Soledad's phone: Thanks for coming!

I can't call Silvia or Raven and break up the celebration. That would be ruining Maribel's big night where she's finally the center of attention. But even if Fernando comes back to the car right now, I'm not letting him drive me anywhere.

I get out of the car. I don't think RydeKids even operates this late. And there's still the chance I could get home without Mom ever knowing I was gone. All I have to do is walk the rest of the way.

"Hey, Eden, hey!" Fernando calls out as I cross the parking lot toward the sidewalk. "No, wait! I'm sorry! We can go!"

I keep walking. "No, we're close. I'll walk." We're not close. I'm not even a hundred percent sure how to get home from here, but I'll figure it out.

"Dude, I'm so sorry. Let me drive you."

"No thanks."

"Eden, I can't let you walk home alone."

"You've been drinking."

He wipes his hand down his face and swears. "I'm sorry, it was only a swallow. I swear I'm good to drive. Look!" He holds out his arms to the sides and then reaches in to touch the tip of his nose—a sobriety test I've seen cops use with drunk drivers on Grandma's crime shows.

He passes. But still.

"No, I'm walking." Of all the decisions I've made tonight, this is the one I'm most sure of.

"Okay, wait, just—"

But I don't wait. I keep walking. Fernando must run back to his car, because a minute later it's crawling along beside me as I walk in what I hope is the right direction.

"I told you, I'm walking!"

"I know," he says through the window. "And I respect that. But I'm going to follow you to be sure you get home okay."

I try to glare, although it's probably too dark for him to see. "But you better not drunk drive into me."

He chuckles. "I promise I'm not drunk, Eden."

We carry on like that, me walking, his car crawling along

behind me. If anyone noticed us, he'd probably look highly suspicious. But that's not my problem.

What is my problem is when Mom's car swerves to a stop in front of Fernando's. I expect her to swoop down on me with the righteous fury of a Greek goddess, but instead, she turns that wrath on Fernando.

"Who the hell are you?" she yells, yanking open his door. "And why are you following my daughter!"

"No, Mom, he's not! I mean, he is! But just to make sure I get home okay."

Fernando stumbles out of the car, and this time he looks drunk, but it's probably because of how my mom is yanking on his arm with her Pilates strength.

"Oh yeah, very chivalrous! You know him?" she asks me.

"Yes, he's . . . he's friends with Maribel's family."

She stares at him. "You're the singer. The big star of that video."

Fernando wisely says nothing in return.

"If you're so trusted, why not let her actually ride inside the car?"

Fernando glances at me, panicked. I don't even want to know what'll happen if I give him up, but I don't have to wonder for long because he does it himself. "Ma'am, I was giving your daughter a ride when I stopped for gas. I happened to see a couple of buddies and one of them offered me a drink."

Mom whips out her phone.

"Ma'am, I only had one swallow, I promise."

"It's true," I say, because as annoyed as I am with Fernando, he made one mistake in the midst of trying to do the right thing.

I can't exactly judge someone for screwing up while having good intentions. "It was one swallow. He's not drunk. But I still knew you wouldn't want me in his car."

"So I was following her, to be sure she got home okay. I am so, so sorry."

Mom takes a slow breath and comes to a decision. "You should be sorry," she says to Fernando. "You don't offer rides to middle school girls whose families don't know you."

"I understand, ma'am. Though respectfully, I don't think leaving her to walk home alone in the dark was the right choice either."

Mom considers him. I know her well enough to know that she respects him standing up for himself in the face of her fury. "Yes, well, everyone's made some poor choices tonight. My daughter included. Eden, get in my car."

"Thank you, Fernando," I mutter.

"Take care, Eden."

Mom is silent all the way home, practically vibrating with rage.

At home, all she says is, "I don't want to say something I'll regret, so we will talk about this in the morning."

Which is probably one of her business tactics. But the end result is that I have an entire night ahead of me to worry about what's coming.

I wake up early, with Blizz curled up on my feet.

"Hey, Blizzy."

At the sound of my voice, he scoots up to my face. He really is the sweetest thing, especially first thing in the morning. His needs are simple—food, shelter, attention. And I haven't even been able to give him that in the time he's lived with me. At least not attention.

Because I've never been a dog person. I didn't ask for him; he just appeared.

Exactly like I appeared in my mom's life, even though all she wanted was to pursue her career. She didn't ask for a kid. Then one was there, along with the responsibilities and distractions of motherhood.

To my surprise, she doesn't wait for me to come downstairs. Normally, all serious talks happen at the kitchen table—I think she's most comfortable in a situation that feels like she's sitting across her desk from an employee.

Instead, she knocks and comes in when I say she can.

"Can I sit?" she asks, and pulls my desk chair over by the bed.

I nod, sitting up and pulling Blizz into my lap.

She takes a deep breath. "When I was your age, I felt so stuck."

Here we go—the story of how she built everything she has to get out of that awful trailer-park life and I should feel grateful. Except that's not where she goes.

"Grandma's happy now, but when my dad was around, they fought all the time. She was pretty miserable. We both were. And that trailer is small. It's not a judgment on how Grandma lives. It's just a fact. You couldn't even cry in the shower without someone hearing you."

I think about Maribel and her house, which seems like a paradise of love and happy family to me, but that she's so desperate to escape (or at least to have her own room).

"I made some stupid choices," Mom says.

"Grandma says you were trouble," I say, and Mom's eyebrows shoot up.

"Does she? She doesn't know the half of it. I had an older boy-friend who was a jerk, but I didn't care because he got me out of there. I didn't even care when he drove drunk."

Now it's my turn to be surprised. More than surprised. Both at what she said and the fact that she's talking to me like this at all.

"Fernando's not my—"

She waves me off. "I know. I talked to Silvia about him last night." She closes her eyes and takes another deep breath. "I stayed with that boyfriend until he crashed the car with me in it."

"Mom! Were you—"

"I was fine. We both walked away with nothing but scratches. Grandma never even knew. But I knew then that not only did I have to get out of there, but I couldn't rely on anyone else to get me out. It had to be me."

It makes sense. It explains a lot about my mom. But that doesn't make it right. "Trusting other people isn't a bad thing."

"No." She gives a sad smile. "You're right about that. But, Eden, I know why I was willing to be so reckless. What I was trying to escape. What I can't figure out is what's so bad here, with me, that you'd risk so much to escape?"

"But that's just it. I've never been trying to escape," I tell her. "I've been trying to find a place where I can be a part of something, where I'm wanted." My voice wobbles.

But it's nothing compared to what her voice does when she says, "Where you're *wanted*?"

"Yes." I'm tempted to back out. But I've already started to run toward this vault. "A place where people want me there, who see what I have to offer, who let me be part of something."

"Honey, I know I work long hours, but—"

"It's not your hours. I mean, it is. But only because I know you'd rather be there than here with me. I know being a businesswoman was your dream, and I'm just an obstacle to it."

"Eden, *no.*"

"I'm like Blizz, just a show dog you didn't even want who got dumped on you, and now I can't even win shiny ribbons."

I can't stop the tears, and I don't even try.

Mom's crying too. "Eden, no. That's completely false. I wanted you. I *want* you. You are the best part of my life, and if I don't show it the way you need me to, that's on me and I need to do better."

I know when Mom is saying something strategically, to get what she needs out of a situation. But this—the emotion in her eyes—is different.

"You wanted me?"

She grabs my hands tight. "I absolutely wanted you. But, honey, listen. Even if you'd been a surprise? You'd still be the best, most important part of my life. I'm going to do better at showing you. I promise. So much you'll probably want me to back off."

A laugh sneaks out between my tears. Then she's laughing too, and Blizz is hopping in between us, unsure what's going on.

If my mom can admit when she's screwed up, then I can too. "I'm sorry for sneaking out and disobeying you."

"Are you?"

"I'm sorry for making you worry, I really am. And for lying. Not only last night." I pause, and my mom waits without feeling the silence. Finally, I say, "But I also feel like you've been really unreasonable."

I brace myself for her response to that. But she actually laughs a little. "You sound like my mother."

"You talked to Grandma about this?"

"Of course I did," she says. "Your father, too. They've both used the word 'unreasonable,' and stronger words besides."

This kind of blows my mind. I know Grandma and Dad always have my back, but it's been sort of like knowing the tumbling mats are there. They might cushion things a tiny bit, but if you fall, it's still going to hurt a ton. It's not that they don't love me a lot, but they're just not here, and Mom is such a force.

It helps to know they're standing up for me when I don't even realize it. Maybe I have more of a team behind me than I thought.

She sighs. "I'm pretty terrible at this mothering thing, aren't I?"

"No, I mean, you've provided this amazing life for me. . . ."

"But it's all just stuff, isn't it? If you don't also have the attention you need. If my moral authority is so weak, you'll put yourself in dangerous situations just to get out from under my thumb."

"I was only at the middle school play," I point out.

"And then riding home with a teenager who ended up drinking?"

"Okay, but I wasn't doing it to rebel. I'd made commitments to people. I'd been working on that show for months, and Maribel needed to know I care about her, even if you don't."

"I never said I don't care about Maribel."

"Only that you don't approve of her. Or her family. Or Will and Raven."

She leans forward and puts her head in her hands. Blizz toddles across the bed and calculates the jump across to her lap.

"I've handled this badly. It felt to me like you didn't respect what I've built, and you didn't care about my approach to menstrual equity. I do have thoughts, you know? I run a menstrual products company. But you preferred to get your information from these people I don't know. You didn't even tell me your period had started!"

It hadn't occurred to me. It's not like my mother was going to throw me a moon party. "I didn't have to. You've always kept my bathroom stocked."

She nods. "But did you tell Maribel and her mom?"

I mean, I was with them when it happened. But she deserves the truth about this, at least.

"You don't owe me every detail of your life as you grow older. I know I haven't done enough to earn your trust. But moving forward, can we both try to communicate more?"

"I'd like that. But also, Mom, my new friends are important to me. And the ballot initiative is important to me. It's not a rebellion against what you stand for. If you have ideas about menstrual equity, maybe we could join forces. But I need you to understand these are good people who deserve your respect. I don't expect you to quit your job and be a stay-at-home mom. But I deserve the freedom to spend time with people I care about, and who care about me." If they'll have me, anyway.

Mom's eyes tear up. "You are a tough negotiator," she says. "I'd like to think you got a little bit of that from me. But I also have a lot to learn from you."

Chapter Twenty-One

Two weeks later Mom and I pull up to Casa Esperanza with a trunk full of MySecret products. Not castoffs, either, but straight out of a shipment of the latest styles.

Maribel runs out and beelines for the car, not to help us unload but to get Blizz out of his harness in the backseat and smother him with kisses. When she first suggested Blizz could hang out at the food bank after school whenever I'm there, Silvia resisted. Dogs and food and hygiene, etc. But Maribel countered with the social media accounts of bodega cats, and promised we'd keep Blizz in the office area anyway.

Silvia agreed to try it once, and then she fell as hard for Blizz as Maribel did. As soon as Maribel sets him down inside, he bounds to the back, where he knows someone will dole out treats from the stash now kept next to the fruit snacks. He's thrilled, Maribel's thrilled, and honestly, so am I. When Blizz has more people lavishing attention on him, he's so much less overwhelming when it's just the two of us at home. I've started to really enjoy the little guy.

Once Mom and I have fully stocked the shelves with MySecret products, we take the leftover into the back.

"We've never had too many menstrual products to stock," Silvia says with delight. She greets my mom graciously and shows her into the classroom.

"Do I have a minute before the meeting?" I ask Soledad, who's sitting at the head of the table.

"Yup."

I take one of the boxes of pads into the bathroom to fill up the bowl on the back of the toilet and snag one to use myself, remembering that first day in this bathroom and the bulky wad of toilet paper I used when I didn't know what else to do.

When I come out, I bump into Will, who's carrying a tray of coffees. One cup with a loose lid sloshes its hot contents and Will almost drops the tray. I reach out to steady the tray, my fingers closing over his.

"Oh my gosh, Will, I'm so sorry!"

We've texted a little over the past couple of weeks, but he hasn't been around Casa Esperanza and he's been "too busy" whenever I've suggested meeting there.

I take the tray from him and set it on a nearby cabinet. He holds his scalding, wet T-shirt away from his skin.

"Hang on," I say, rushing into the bathroom and grabbing a handful of paper towels. I bring them back and thrust them at him, not wanting to overstep and wipe him up myself.

He takes them and holds them to the wet spot, absorbing what he can.

"I'm so sorry, I wasn't looking where I was going, I'm such a klutz—"

"Eden, hey. Relax."

A strangled laugh escapes my throat. Relax?

"Sorry," he says, with a snort of his own laughter. "You don't really do relaxed, do you?"

He's not wrong. Whether I'm trying to reach the highest levels of an elite sport or make as many pads as possible or get an amendment on a ballot I can't even vote on, I kind of only have one mode: code red.

But some things can't be forced. Sometimes, no matter how hard you work, you don't make it to the Olympics. No matter how many pads you sew, you're not solving the problems of period poverty. And no matter how much I want to make things better with Will, it might just be too late.

"I'm sorry." I step back to give him space. "I'll take the drinks in to the meeting."

But he stops me. "Thanks," he says. "It's nice to not be the klutz for once."

I give him a tentative smile. "I'll spill coffee on you anytime."

And there it is: the full-wattage smile I haven't seen on Will's face for weeks. "Look, Eden, I know it might seem like I overreacted—"

"You didn't."

"Just . . . let me say this. I don't trust easily. It's not safe for me to trust everyone. But I'm working on trusting the people who deserve it." I nod. I can't ask for anything more. Which is why I'm shocked when he adds, "I think you deserve it."

I set the tray of drinks back down. "I want to deserve it." I step close, maybe too close. And then for some reason I take the wad of coffee-stained paper towels from his hand. It's intimate, like a parent letting a kid spit gum into their hand. I take the paper towels into the bathroom and toss them, giving myself a second to gather myself.

"I'm going to mess up," I tell him when I return, and he's still there, waiting for me. "I'm working on messing up, actually," I tell him. "I've spent a lot of years doing everything perfectly."

"Well, you made a really good start," he says, with a sparkle in his eye. "Gold medal job of messing up."

I bump his shoulder with my shoulder. "Surely not gold. Bronze, maybe?"

He bumps me back. "Okay, bronze."

I carry the tray of drinks into the classroom, and as I step through the doorway, Will pats my shoulder. Soledad's watching our every move and quirks a single perfect eyebrow at me before moving to begin the meeting.

She, Verity, and Cole are at one end of the table. Silvia, Maribel, and Raven are at the other end of the table. Mom's in the middle. I go to sit next to my mom, and Will sits across from us.

"All right, come to order, Team Hashtag Code Red," Soledad says. "Welcome to Heather Sorensen, CEO of MySecret. Why don't we introduce ourselves, so Heather can get to know the team?"

Once introductions have been made, Cole hands out a spreadsheet showing the signatures that have been gathered so far, from all the different cities across the state.

"This is amazing," my mother says.

"Honestly, Eden's video made all the difference," Soledad says.

"It wasn't my—"

Soledad cuts me off. "It was your idea, and you need to start owning that."

My mother considers Soledad, and I know she's about to offer her a job on the spot.

I look at the total numbers at the bottom of the spreadsheet. "So we're at . . . 332,420? Isn't that over our goal?"

"It's over the required number," Verity says. "But remember that we want to shoot for twenty percent more, in case of fake names or unregistered voters."

"Right."

"We still have two weeks," Soledad says. "And Fernando reached out to Madison Cho to see if she'll record another duet with him for a final push. We're waiting to hear on that."

Mom cuts a glance at me. "Fernando from that night?"

I nod. "He's a good guy, I promise."

"So now we're excited to hear from Heather about her ideas around how we can partner with MySecret."

It seems absurd, partnering with the big corporation on an initiative to tax the big corporations. But then again, my mom's whole job has to do with menstruation.

"Thanks so much to everyone for having me," she says, looking around the table. "I know I was a bit closed off at first, and I'm grateful for your grace. And that you've all been good friends to Eden."

She clears her throat and then goes on. "You're nearly there on the signatures, so it seems almost certain you'll get this initiative on the ballot. In all honesty, our normal course of action would be to launch a sophisticated campaign urging voters to vote no on something that's going to raise our tax burden. But you all are innovating, and I think we need to as well.

"I've already spoken with our legal team and we will not be fighting against the initiative." Soledad lets out a little squeal. "What's more, if it gets on the ballot, I'd like to propose another video. A television ad this time—I can't sing, but I can offer the MySecret resources, and I would be willing to appear in the video, giving MySecret's support to the initiative."

"Not bad advertisement for you," Will observes.

"Will!" Maribel throws a wadded-up fruit-snack wrapper at him.

"No, he's right," Mom says. "It is. I'm still a businesswoman." Will nods, like he might be able to respect that. "I've also got a team working on a proposal for each MySecret distribution center to partner with a local food bank in their area to give a monthly supply of product. And once we've figured out the kinks, we'd share the approach with the other menstrual products companies and peer pressure them to do something similar." She looks around the table. "How does that sound?"

"I think it sounds pretty great," Raven says, turning to Soledad, who nods so hard, I'm afraid her giant hoop earrings might fly out of her ears.

"I tell you what," Will says, leaning back in his chair. "You're not nearly as ferocious as Eden made you out to be."

Everyone freezes for an agonizing second, until my mother throws back her head and laughs.

"Oh! Oh! Oh!" Cole jumps up, showing more emotion than I've ever seen from them and quieting down everyone's laughs. "I heard from Fernando! Madison Cho is in!"

The laughter turns to cheers. Maribel and I lock eyes and say at the exact same time, "Thank Frank!" and everyone looks at us like we're total weirdos and we are, which is great, and everyone's hugging and Blizz is barking and I can't believe how much my world has changed over the past few months.

We're not there yet—two more weeks to go. But with this many people working together, it's almost certain we'll get the initiative—*my* initiative—on the ballot, and with MySecret's support, it has a real chance of passing.

Maybe it won't. Nothing's certain. I thought for so many years that I knew what the next ten years of my life would be—junior elite, senior elite, world championships, Olympics—if I did everything in my control to make it happen. But too many things were out of my control, as it turned out. The dream didn't die, it changed.

The initiative's fate isn't in my control now. It never was. All I can do is fight my hardest to make it happen. And if it doesn't? Then I adjust the dream. Find a new way to fight. A new way to win.

A new way to make my voice heard for the things that matter.

Author's Note

I got my first period when I was twelve. I remember it vividly, because I was wearing white jeans, at a beach bonfire with my cousins—all boys. They didn't notice, and I had both an older sister and a mom with supplies and advice to share. It's a pretty tame first period story.

My close friend, however, got her first period at school in seventh grade. It soaked through her skirt, and to complicate things, she was blind, so she didn't realize what had happened. A boy noticed and—I am forever grateful to him—told her discreetly and walked her to the nurse's office.

That boy was an ally—someone who doesn't experience something themself, but shows up to help and support those who are going through it, without making it about themself.

Talking about menstruation isn't as taboo today as it was when I was kid, and thank goodness! But there are still challenges. Menstruators who don't identify as girls face some of the biggest challenges. Think about it: Even if your school provides menstrual products, they're probably in the girls' bathroom, right? What about boys like Will?

People living in poverty, which included nearly 11 million American children as of 2021 (americanprogress.org), have a very difficult time paying for menstrual supplies, and sometimes miss school or work because of their periods. Eighty-four percent of young menstruators experience painful periods, and thirty-two percent of them miss school or work because of the pain (*Journal of Pain Research*, https://www.ncbi.nlm.nih.gov/pmc/articles/PMC3392715/).

I don't mention these things to scare you, especially if you haven't had a period! For most people, the discomfort is manageable and periods are just an inconvenience you get used to (if you're fortunate enough to be able to afford the supplies you need). But I mention them because the more we talk about things, the closer we get to solutions. Wonderful organizations (like the fictional Periods with Dignity) are doing this work so that free menstrual products are available for those who need them, in the United States and around the world. Countries like Japan, Spain, and Indonesia offer menstruating employees the right to two additional days off of work each month. Scotland offers free menstrual products for all in community centers and pharmacies.

How Can You Help?

Does your school provide free menstrual products for anyone who needs them? If you live in California, New York, Illinois, New Hampshire, Virginia, Oregon, or Washington, your state law requires schools to provide them. (Though, as in Washington, the law might not supply the funds to do so, which is a problem.) As of this writing, bills related to menstrual equity have been introduced in thirty-seven states.

You can find local organizations already doing this work and volunteer your time with them, boost their social media posts, and encourage your parents to support them financially, if they're able. You could lead a charge in your own school or community to make sure period products are available for those who need them.

If you're not a menstruator, I'm especially glad you read this book. Our world gets better the more we understand the experiences of people whose lives are different from our own. You can stand with your menstruating peers in advocating for menstrual equity and against period poverty in your schools and communities. You can speak up if someone is getting bullied because of their period, and you can educate those around you on how to use more inclusive language, such as saying "menstruator" instead of referring to "girls" and "women" as those who menstruate. You can even keep menstrual products in your backpack or locker and let your menstruating friends know you've got them if they need anything.

Whether you're a menstruator or not, one of the biggest things you can do is to normalize periods. It's a monthly part of life for half the humans on the planet, and the more we talk about it without shame, the better for everyone!

Some Terms to Understand

Menstruator: A person born with ovaries and a uterus, who experiences a regular menstrual cycle.

Menstrual cycle: The cycle of the reproductive system of people with uteruses, which is usually about twenty-eight days long. This cycle results in a period, during which blood and tissue flow out of the body for, on average, three to five days.

Menstrual equity: Making menstrual products accessible, affordable, and safe for all who need them; making sure that people understand their options and the best way to stay healthy.

Period poverty: The struggle to afford menstrual products, and the loss of education or work opportunities because of an inability to afford those products.

Additional Resources
Fiction

Go with the Flow by Lily Williams and Karen Schneemann

The Moon Within by Aida Salazar

Revenge of the Red Club by Kim Harrington

Grow Up, Tahlia Wilkins! by Karina Evans

Nonfiction

Puberty Is Gross but Also Really Awesome by Gina Loveless

Period Power: A Manifesto for the Menstrual Movement by Nadya Okamoto

Red Moon Gang: An Inclusive Guide to Periods by Tara Costello

Welcome to Your Period! by Yumi Stynes and Dr. Melissa Kang

Some Menstrual Movement Organizations

Period. (www.period.org): Founded by a teen!

#HappyPeriod (www.hashtaghappyperiod.org): The first Black-led menstrual equity organization.

Free The Tampons (wwww.freethetampons.org): Working to make menstrual products free in all bathrooms.

The Pad Project (www.thepadproject.org): Bringing machines and the training to use them around the world, so communities can make their own reusable pads.

Days for Girls International (www.daysforgirls.org): If you sew, like Eden, you can join a local chapter and make cloth pads through Days for Girls!

Documentary Film

Period. End of Sentence (2018), directed by Rayka Zehtabchi.

Acknowledgments

First and foremost, my thanks to my wonderful editor, Reka Simonsen, who came to me with the idea that there might be a middle grade novel around the work done by Days for Girls International. That was the seed of *Code Red*; it would not exist without her suggestion.

Never-ending thanks to my agent Jim McCarthy, whose unflagging support means the world.

The wonderful team at Atheneum including Kristie Choi, Jeannie Ng, Rebecca Syracuse, and Elizabeth Blake-Linn. Thank you for taking my words in a document and making them into a beautiful book that readers can hold.

Many thanks to Rochelle Deans for being my gymnastics guru, and to A. J. Sass for your thoughtful reading of Will's character. Any faults are my own. Thanks to pelvic floor physical therapist Simone Romero at Flow Rehab in Seattle for insightful, gender-sensitive discussions of menstrual issues. Thanks to Kate Hawk-Ritenauer at Seattle T2P2 (Towers of Tampons and Pyramids of Pads) for discussing menstrual equity advocacy. You can donate to support their efforts here: https://www.seattlet2p2.org/.

My mom, for teaching me how to sew.

And my family, as always, for cheering me on every step of the way: thank you, thank you, thank you!